A Novel of Mid-Century San Francisco

ANN MARY, CONTRACEPTION AND THE POPE OF ROME

Nancy Taforo-Murphy

Ann Mary, Contraception and the Pope of Rome copyright © 2016 Nancy Taforo-Murphy.

All rights reserved under International and Pan-American Copyright Conventions. No part of this book may be used or reproduced in any manner without prior written permission.

First print edtion.

Printed in the United States of America.

Ann Mary, Contraception and the Pope of Rome is a work of fiction. Any resemblance to persons living or dead is coincidental and unintended.

Book and cover design by
Patrick Gallagher, Green Isles Press,
California, USA.

Cover photograph licensed by Getty Images.

"…every action which, whether in anticipation of the conjugal act, or in its accomplishment, or in the development of its natural consequences, proposes, whether as an end or as a means, to render procreation impossible is intrinsically evil."

Catechism of the Catholic Church

1995

"Most of the greatest evils that man has inflicted upon man have come through people feeling quite certain about something which, in fact, was false."

Unpopular Essays

Bertrand Russell

1950

PROLOGUE

My mother sat on a wooden toilet seat in a cold, porcelain-tiled lavatory, parted her legs and swabbed at the cleft beyond her pubic hair. Gingerly, cautiously, and with great trepidation, she slid the toilet paper forward, and for a moment her body functions, physical, mental, and certainly emotional, were suspended, balanced on a cusp of expectation and dread. She examined the paper. Would there be a smear of red, a bit of clotted tissue releasing blood like an inky feathery tracery on blotting paper? Or would there be no red, only the pale yellow ordinariness of pee? My mother made this wrenching examination every month, made necessary by the total prohibition of contraceptives by her church. The blood was to her salvation, and in some convoluted way, the blood of an unborn child, the child she was profoundly grateful that she would never bear, deliver or care for, the blood of her own release and survival.

This is my mother's story as it was witnessed by me, her daughter Teresa Kenny, then, and as it was told to me later. This is the story of Ann Mary Kenny as it happened against the background of Catholic parish life in San Francisco in the years just after World War II.

FATHER CAPWELL AND SEX

SEX, NASTY WORD, FATHER CAPWELL OUR PASTOR THOUGHT. All those words, sex, pecker, prick, the pox, some words were just better off not said. Why, there were some women, ladies like his own dear mater, a saintly mother to nine children, or, certainly, like his Aunt Bertha, a maiden for her 86 years, who probably went through their whole lives without saying it. And here was this woman on the phone, a Mrs. Kenny, breaking the bounds of propriety and asking him for an interview on that very topic. Well, to be sure, she hadn't quite said the word, but it was implied. And even in this year of 1946, in the City of San Francisco, swarming with soon-to-be-discharged sailors and soldiers, such talk was still deplorable. All these unseemly words rampaged through the poor priest's brain. His head spun.

For Father Capwell was less than happy. Into this cold foggy morning, too early for polite telephone calls, had come the jingle ring of the black Bakelite phone. He had just re-entered the rectory from Mass, taken off his coat and positioned himself, cassock skirt slightly lifted in front of the steaming radiator when he heard the demanding ring. The lady on the line, identifying herself as Mrs. Kenny, asked in an urgent voice if she and her husband could see him that evening. She was snuffling in a very inappropriate manner. She went on at length, rambling as many ladies did, every other sentence an apology, and broached on some topics that did not seem, to the easily embarrassed priest, respectful of polite society. He scribbled the name down, Mrs. Ann Kenny, and her husband, Henry, not a Catholic as he remembered it, a fellow he had seen at the children's baptisms, a fellow with a sour mug.

Oh, why had he picked up the phone, he chided himself. That was certainly a major character fault on his part, he admitted, his impetuosity. Why had he not left it to his housekeeper, Mrs. Heafy, to answer? She would have taken care of it in short order, that was for sure. Now here he was, the pastor, the chief shepherd of and caretaker to the souls of St. Cyril's, having to come up with difficult answers to a bothersome woman on a subject of great indelicacy. Certainly his station should spare him that. He stooped over laboriously and opening the cupboard door, found, under the telephone book, the envelope of important papers. Riffling through the yellowed sheets, he saw what he was looking for.

> "The successor of Jesus Christ who is God was Peter and Peter's successor is the Pope. Now would God want any successor of his to be able to make a mistake about what people can rightly do or not? And so the Pope cannot make such a mistake. This exemption from error is called infallibility."

Father Capwell had penned that in his schoolboy cursive, the first year that he was in seminary when he was only 15, his copy sheet scattered with plump, rounded d's and g's and wobbly l's and f's. But it was sincere, heartfelt writing and he did not disown it. It always calmed him down, and clarified his rather swimmy mental processes, and helped him do what he hated most, face inquiring parishioners. Father had certainly applied himself to the study of church law, but it had not entirely succeeded in making him sufficiently insensible to the distress of others. He admitted to himself that he didn't really know the ins and outs of philosophical speculations, but you couldn't expect a streetcar conductor to know all about the history of transportation, or a plumber to be an expert on the Roman baths, now could you? He was though, he reminded himself, as he had been coached in seminary, God's representative on earth, and, like a trickle of water through a corroded pipe, some small part of that certitude, that infallibility, must be his. Or so he hoped. For he was a man of rigid ritual, sanctified hands, poorly kept ledgers (a gross of votive candles was $16.72, but how much for each one?), and memorized answers to cosmic questions. He was a good man, no dispute there.

Father Capwell that evening waited for Mr. and Mrs. Kenny, pacing up and down in the room he liked to call, in a rare attempt at pretentiousness, his study, but which Mrs. Heafy, in customary obstinacy, called his back room. It was a study in that it housed a podium, discarded by the nuns, where Father practiced his sermons, such as they were, and his few beloved books. But also housed were Mrs. Heafy's ironing board, stacks of old *Limerick Gazettes* sent to him by a dutiful sister in that city, and a collection of slightly broken furniture, too good to throw away, chairs with three good legs, one gamey, and school desks whose lids just might murderously give way. Here Father felt comfortable among familiar things: in the closet were the fishing waders (never used), bought at no small expense for Peter Paul by his father, and the carton of light bulbs, meant for City Hall, each one marked with a delicate stamp, "Property of the City and County of San Francisco," and donated by a generous former parishioner. In his "study" Father Capwell could station himself behind the lump of a wooden desk, the cleaning of which, he admitted to himself, would be like polishing a turd. In the dim light of the cluttered room he felt secure and he hoped his explanations would be taken with appropriate docility.

Mrs. Kenny, my mother, wearing her best gabardine suit, skirt seat shiny from too many wears, jacket still presentable, entered and sat anxiously before him like a sparrow on a tremulous twig, hoping to elicit from Father some dispensation from the ironclad prohibition against the use of artificial contraceptives. Her husband, almost lost in the dim reaches of the room, preferred, it seemed, not to sit down.

Father Capwell spoke first, opening the dog-eared manual before him, *Brief Answers to Life's Profound Questions*. Oh, how much Father owed the author, Eamon Sweeney, Primate of Witchita, Kansas for his authoritative guidance on the eternal verities. When Father Capwell needed help on such matters, he had to reach no further than his *Brief Answers*. With Sweeney at his side, he could handle anything.

"From what you told me on the telephone, Mrs. Kenny, I believe the following passage will set all things right:

> 'Oneness, permanence, and the possibility of fertility must characterize the holy marriage. Polygamy contradicts oneness, divorce denies

> permanence, and the interference with fertility makes impossible God's greatest gift, the child.'"

Father turned brightly to the two visitors, "There you have it."

And Mr. Kenny's voice came to him from the dark corner, "Does it say anything there, Father, about bestiality – having a hankering after goats?"

Oh, this was not a good beginning at all, thought Father Capwell. Such irreverence. Better to feign a hard of hearing than to answer. He would take another approach. He fumbled for the necessary passage.

> "Every action, in connection with the conjugal act, which proposes to render procreation impossible, is intrinsically evil."

"Do you see?" Father said, pleading this time, the brightness gone from his voice. If truth be known, he felt very uncomfortable saying these things. Even conditioned as he was from early childhood in the legalisms of the Catholic Church, the words stuck in his mouth in the saying of them, dry and brittle and without humanity. He had utterly failed in the fastidious indifference that other priests had so well mastered, full of stale evasions, insincere assurances, and false smiles. No wonder the woman sat before him, uncomprehending as if he were speaking some sort of Slovenian. In his heart of hearts, he didn't blame her.

Father continued, the words tumbling out of his mouth, repeating what had been drummed into his head. "Now the great St. Thomas Aquinas wrote a book in 12 something or other, the *Summa Theologica* which is still our guide. He said that if the primary purpose of an act is confounded, then that goes against God's natural law which is, as we know, a mortal sin."

Mrs. Kenny's face screwed up in a real effort to understand what St. Thomas knew about her plight. Trying to wrest some sort of compassion and understanding from Mother Church, she rubbed her corded forehead, pushing her dime-store hat askew. Her anxiety far outstripped her vanity. "But you see, Father, I already have three children."

"And a fine family that, though a bit on the small side," Father Capwell answered with the best he could do of a hearty chuckle.

"But the oldest is 11, that's Virginia, and then there's the middle one, Teresa, and the little one, Freddy, and since then I've had two miscarriages, you see I'm doing my best, and it's so hard to time things right, even when the...," and here her voice trailed off for decency's sake.

At the mention of "miscarriages," Father Capwell did flinch inwardly. Into his mind careened, though stop it he tried, the child Peter Paul at the bottom of the steep farmhouse stairs, hearing his mother's knife-like screams, and his Aunt Bertha, her arms full of blood stained rags, brushing by him on the way to the scullery. He felt small and full of anguish.

But back to the brief answers, back to the eternal verities, "You're getting into particulars, Mrs. Kenny, particulars. The majesty of the Church requires that we take the long view. We must never lose sight of the eternal principles. Now, what if God and the Church made an exception in your case, now you could see where that would land us, don't you?" Father too was imploring now and both persons sat, bodies straining across the small expanse of the desk, across the huge divide between the theological absolutes and the exigencies and curses of everyday life, in the semi-darkness of the ill lit room, yearning to be understood.

"Where would that lead?" came the husband's voice, "to a great deal more common sense, that's where," and then followed a disgusted, "Jesus Christ," to the horror of Mrs. Kenny and Father Capwell.

"Don't mind that, Father. It's just a little prayer," and he laughed a bitter laugh.

But the priest had an inspiration. This would clinch the argument in his favor. "We are called to live as St. Joseph lived. Pure not only in mind, but pure in body."

"Cock and bull, Father."

Father Capwell stiffened. "You must grasp the nettle, Mr. Kenny," and the priest was immediately horrified by the tone and the Englishness of what he had said.

"And you can push that nettle up your ass, Father," Mr. Kenny said as he left the room.

Poor Father Capwell. Never had he ever imagined a conversation proceeding like this. He sat bewildered and my mother wept.

FATHER CAPWELL AND THE CATHOLIC FAITH

WHEN FATHER CAPWELL THOUGHT ABOUT IT AT ALL, which was almost never, he thought of Jesus as a decent sort, a country man, a digger of potatoes perhaps, a man who could take a rainstorm and not grumble, a man who would if he could, and sure he could, he was God, wasn't he, would have a dog – the dogless life the biggest drawback, as Father Capwell saw it, to being a priest and not in the domestic state. But when the other clerics talked on and on about Jesus, they let on about the sun and the palm trees, maybe even camels, and the other men with swarthy complexions and it sort of took the shine off it. If truth be known, Father Capwell didn't give much truck to the Jesus side of Christianity, other than the rules and precepts and forbidden things, though he did like the Blessed Virgin Mary, everyone likes a pretty woman, and the dozens of statuettes littering his parlor all attested to the prettiness of the B.V.M. Of that he had no doubt.

On the contrary, some of the nuns, well, he didn't know where they got them – probably utterly unmarriageable and so they got convented off – an unworthy thought though none the less true. He did try to mentally pummel down such considerations when he talked to Sister Constance with her protruding, pointy chin finished off with a ruddy mole, and that topped off with a quavering hair. But it was to the Father, the Godhead, that Peter Paul Capwell mostly addressed his prayers because that seemed most plausible – his own father having been unpredictable, given to rare, solitary, inexplicable kindnesses, but also very often to cruelty. It fit in well with Father Capwell's idea of the fatherhood of God.

Digging in his small plot of sandy earth at the side of the rectory, Father Capwell forgot his cares, chief among them being the distressing interview the evening before with his parishioner, Mrs. Kenny, and her disrespectful husband. Father's vegetable garden was one of the hundreds of Victory Gardens planted across the city, at the urging of F.D.R., their beloved president. It was Father's pride and joy. Every single one of his lady parishioners was happy to accept the dirty paper bags, heavy with parsnips, turnips, carrots and his favorite, potatoes. Father liked to imagine the happy families, especially the children, gratefully sitting down to a steaming bowl of vegetable soup. Though the war was over, the Victory Garden was still the one thing in life that the priest was fussy about – that people keep out of his patch and there was a proper fence and a sign telling them to do so. He slid the spade into the earth, a pleasing slice, and ruminated on potatoes. Ah spuds, boiled, then forked mashed, salt and pepper, with a bit of cream and lots of butter. He closed his eyes and tilted his head back, almost tasting the salty butter glazing his lips.

He was not above putting his potatoes into his sermons, in a timely and appropriate way of course. "We are all imperfect, just as the lowly potato is not perfect – some with eyes, some with a bit of mold, but good in the eating just the same." The whole subject of potatoes, in fact, reminded him that the earth is kind and God's creatures on it. He got more comfort from that, to be sure, than from dwelling on the Incarnation.

Father Capwell, satisfied with his labors, put his shovel away. His life was a simple one. The 6:30 Mass to get that out of the way, a little time in his garden, a visit to the school, the daily reading of the Breviary, and the few calls paid on cranky elderly parishioners, their houses smelling, as his did, of damp wallpaper and unopened windows. His advice to them often was to cultivate a special saint – his own was St. Anne. She had always been his favorite – nothing showy about her, no swoons or fits or spectacular stigmata, just a kind older sister watching out for you. And then there were the semi-deities assigned to a special plight – St. Blaise for ailments of the throat, St. Lucy for eye trouble, St. Julia for gastric problems, wind and the like, and those saints who handily had multiple functions like St. Stephen, the patron saint of headache sufferers, stonemasons and, he often left this off, coffin makers. Finally, as tactfully as he could suggest, there was St. Joseph for a happy death.

Today his spirits lifted even more as he thought of his afternoon line of duties, last among them being a visit to the bedridden octogenarian, Mr. Boyle, for their weekly game of checkers. Seated at the invalid's bed, Father Capwell sized up the unblinking black gimlet-eyed skeletal figure half smothered in untidy bed covers. Father was resolved to win. But the skintight twig-like hands shot out from under the sheets, seeming to know exactly where to move his checker pieces to stymie Father Capwell. Game after desperate game, it was not to be. But Father Capwell was an optimist. Next week, if Boyle lasts that long, I'll pummel that gloating, self-important prat, he promised himself.

Conveniently remembering the time, Father Capwell hurried back to the rectory, cassock flapping, breath coming fast and forced. It was almost 5:30 and that meant dinner time, hungry or not, otherwise engaged, or not. Mrs. Heafy had ordained it. Why of all the doting women in his parish did he get that belligerent widow as his housekeeper?

"It's not every man who gets a three course meal for his dinner," she announced most nights. He did not say to himself, all the irritations of married life and none of the comforts, but he felt it in his bones. He thought of what was to come: Campbell soup (it was true that he sometimes got to pick one of two varieties), the meatloaf or roast tormented in her oven into grey slabs so hard on his sore gums, and the Byrd's Custard, a sweet gruel. He could not force himself to be grateful.

"Mrs. Heafy, could I have a bowl without a chip?" He had invaded the pantry, her territory, one day when she had been shopping, a dangerous thing to do, and counted the bowls, all five of them, three chipped, two not.

"It's already poured," she said, as she sloshed the soup bowl down before him.

"Bless us, O Lord, and these Thy gifts which we are about to receive from Thy bounty, through Christ Our Lord, Amen," mumbled Father Capwell, a very patient man.

Finishing his meal, he said to a skeptical Mrs. Heafy, "I'm off to my room to do a little paper work." There he was happy, lying on the bed on his back in his pajamas, running his eyes over the ceiling cracks, as he listened to the radio – the "nettle up your ass" comment of the night before successfully paved over by the scratchy voices from the wooden console – ball games (the San Francisco Seals or the Oakland Oaks, it hardly mattered), or "The Adventures of Sam Spade," or "Stand By For Crime," or "The Bing Crosby Show" (Father took pride – Bing was a Catholic), or his favorite, "The Jack Benny Program." How he loved the man, always poker faced, but always someone's muggins, endlessly put upon by everyone, even his colored valet, Rochester. Father Capwell's spirits soared. Then a little wash-up, dentures in a glass, evening prayers on his knees bedside, and in between the covers early. Ah, the holy life.

THE STENCH FROM HER MOUTH

MY MOTHER ALWAYS AWAKENED US WITH A KISS and a tender little shaking of our shoulders, saying our special morning names: "Bunny" for Virgie, "Sweetie" for me and in the other room, we heard her sing out to Freddy, "Atta Boy, Atta Boy, morning's come."

Soon there was the mush on the stove, boiling up, snapping, sinking into craters. Then the cream, if we were lucky, was poured into our bowls off the top of the freshly opened milk bottle, before the glass quart was given its vigorous shake to mix the cream with the skim. Mom spooned the porridge into Freddy's mouth as he sat banging his grubby little hands on the highchair tray. She then made sure that Virgie, my older sister, and I were presentable for school, wiping off our milk moustaches and tidying our hair and our sailor blouses and Navy blue sweaters. The brush slid easily through Virgie's straight dark hair, but the comb stuck time and time again on the snarls of my curls, matted by sleep into knots. "Ouch, ouch, ouch," I roared. Dad barged into the small kitchen, shouting, "Who was playing with my slide rule again. I left it right here," before mom found it stuck this time in his accounts book. Virgie would moan that she wanted jelly in her peanut butter sandwich, and Mom would answer for the hundredth time that jam was not off the ration book; she'd just have to wait. The radio blared the "Don McNeill's Breakfast Hour jingle, "The March Around the Breakfast Table." Sometimes when things were jolly we'd march together round the table. That was when Dad was feeling good. He was the family's thermostat. Set high, we felt fine. Set low, and our happiness, like the cozy temperature, drained away. In any case we began each day in an uproar.

Our school day went by neither fast nor slow; time seemed static, motionless as the cheaply framed religious pictures on the schoolroom walls: St. Agatha for all time being stoned while protecting her virginity; St. Sebastian caught frozen, as in a stuck newsreel frame, with a hundred arrows flying at his soft, vulnerable body; and St. Agnes waiting, her head on a block, for the executioner's merciful, downward swing. These images were, undeniably, part of our religion.

Below the pictures was the blackboard and on the blackboard today was a paragraph carefully written by Sister Raymond with the goal of our edification, sanctification, and good manners. She read the passage to us and instructed us to copy it in our workbooks.

The Stench from Her Mouth

> "In 1883 a servant girl who had charge of children, used to curse and teach the children to curse. God punished her. She soon suffered fearful pains in her mouth which was full of disgusting sores; they caused her so much pain hat she howled like a beast, and no one could stand the stench from her mouth."

"Teresa Kenny, stop your daydreaming," Sister Raymond demanded sharply. I had been looking around the classroom at the other school girls dressed as I was in ink-stained, soiled middy blouses. I felt the inside of my mouth with my tongue. Dread of the fate threatened by the Commentary gripped me. I feared the worst. I stared goggle-eyed at the hinged square blue sailor collar hanging down the back of the girl in front of me. My jaw slacked stupidly as I probed behind the teeth, between the check and palate and into the gummy craters and gullies of my mouth, and found – to my enormous relief – no horrible surprises, no sores. The surprise would have been great indeed because I – at ten – had never said a naughty word.

"Stop your wool-gathering, Teresa!" Sister Raymond once again admonished me. The nun swept down the narrow classroom aisle, her heavy black cape dusting the desktops on each side. She was beleaguered, always on the alert for malingering and impertinence, weary in the effort of taming the 50 children in her room. Her instructions came out crisp and mandatory. "First two lines of spirals and then copy the Commentary from the blackboard in your best Palmer Method Cursive. Dip your pen sparingly. No ink blots allowed," she instructed.

I lowered my head over my tablet. Diligence consumed me. "Very good, Teresa, very good." She patted my shoulder, delighted that someone cared about the fine points of penmanship as much as she did. But as she spoke, a sour smell wafted over her teeth, teeth coated with something, not as hygienic as toothpaste nor as wholesome as porridge, but some film secreted by an unwell body. I flinched and pulled away just short of being rude. Was that what was called the stench from her mouth? Of what sins was Sister Raymond herself guilty?

The good nun lingered a bit longer and, leaning over, whispered in my ear, "How is your mother, Teresa?"

I felt my face screw up. I didn't know the right answer. What were the neighbors saying? What had my mother done wrong? "She's fine, Sister. She's fine."

"Well, I know you love your mother very much and I know her children are the most important thing in the world to her."

I said nothing. I knew that the most important person in my world was my mother, but the most important thing in my mother's world was the Catholic Church. I was determined to please her though the road to our religion was complicated, fraught with danger signs: go back, proceed with caution, bumpy pavement ahead. Which meant no curse words, no bad companions, no occasions of sin. I would do my best to please my mother, though it was apparent even then that her needs were far beyond my childish reach.

MATHEMATICAL CATHOLICISM

A Chalice

3 Theological Virtues
9 Choirs of Angels
14 Stations of the Cross
5 Wounds of Christ
7 Corporal Works of Mercy
7 Spiritual Works of Mercy
10 Commandments of God
6 Commandments of the Church
7 Last Words on the Cross
12 Articles of the Creed
3 Religious Vows
7 Sacraments
8 Beatitudes
7 Cardinal Sins
7 Principal Virtues
5 Joyful Mysteries of the Rosary
5 Sorrowful Mysteries of the Rosary
5 Glorious Mysteries of the Rosary
4 Last Things, and, finally,
1,500,000,000 Angels on Earth, 1 for every person

DR. SEITZ AND THE RHYTHM METHOD

DR. SEITZ WAS A STARCHED MAN, in clothing, in conversation, in posture and in temperament. His straight hair was combed back and up from his forehead in a permanent military-like attention, his light blue eyes glinted through his metal frame glasses. It was the kind of face that had been scrubbed and scrubbed again.

He sat there behind the protective barrier of his tidy desk and regarded the small woman before him. Once very pretty, he was sure. But now, bedraggled, distracted. Three live births in ten years, two miscarriages. She had asked Dr. Seitz to talk to her husband. Of course he would not. He was not a counselor, nor an abettor of priests and ministers. He had fled from Germany to Britain during the war, and had become acquainted with the punitive nature of Christian doctrine. Jesus holding the lamb. That was a laugh. That was only a sentimental trapping used to camouflage their beliefs, which were a load of codswallop. He had to suppress a smile, thinking of that. The British were quite good at the colloquial – codswallop – nonsense, rubbish, and in the end, drivel. No, he would not talk to her priests or her husband, who he understood was not a Catholic. What in the world could he say to him?

Now the woman was talking. Something about going over the Catholic approved rhythm method of birth control again.

These Catholics! Even backwoods Baptists and orthodox Jews allowed their women modern contraceptives. He had many women patients like her, snuffling, anxious, overworked, almost all of them Catholics, all seeking for a way, within the framework of the Church's prohibitions, to limit their families. They desired from an imprecise method, Vatican roulette, a precise result – no conception. And most of them failed.

This woman, Mrs. Kenny, was afraid, afraid of him, afraid of her Church, afraid of a supposedly benevolent God. Dr. Seitz, a man of science and an atheist, feared little – he viewed the inevitable end of his life, no, call it what it was, his death, with stoic resignation. Something these people who claimed to put their trust in a hereafter and a kind deity, could not do.

Within him warred concern for his patient and annoyance with her, and the annoyance won out. He looked down his very long nose, along his long extended arm in its white lab coat to his aristocratic hand, with its long fingers like jointed chopsticks, holding an elegant pen. He leaned back in the chair. He felt it important that his posture not be misread as empathetic.

"Mrs. Kenny, as I have told you before, to find out the first fertile day, use the shortest cycle in your records. Subtract 18 from the total number of days in that cycle. Now, Mrs. Kenny, please remember that the cycle is from the first day of your bleeding to the next bleeding. To carry on, count from the first day of the cycle and that day is your first fertile day. Say, the shortest cycle is 26 days, subtract 18 from 26 which gives you 8. Now your fertile time starts on day 8. Now, to predict the last day of your fertility, use the longest cycle that you have had in the last 6 months and subtract 11 days from the total.

So, let's do that, 34 minus 11 equals 23. Count 23 days down from the first day of your cycle and that day is the last day of your fertility. So you may not have sexual relations from day 8 to day 23. Ah, but there is another factor: the length of the sperm's viability. It's usually 72 hours, but, it has come to recent knowledge, that some men's sperm last significantly longer. Do you see?"

Mrs. Kenny who was of that generation of women who felt it was their constant obligation to smile and say yes, smiled and said yes. She had only a remote grasp of what the doctor was saying.

Dr. Seitz pushed his calculations across the desk towards her. She leaned forward, head bowed, and stared at the doctor's spidery notations, delicate numbers and letters, stringing across the page like algebraic formulations. She saw them as blindly as an Egyptologist would have seen his first hieroglyphics carved into stone, knowing their importance, but at the same time being baffled by their unintelligibility. She stared long enough for them to blur and dance, or so the tears filling her eyes seemed to make them do.

"You should be very aware of the uncertainties of the rhythm method. These calculations can be radically altered by bodily fluctuations: an illness, a fever, a medication, changes in climate. And, of course, emotional upset. And so if the schedule of your period is not as predicted, it could result in your having sexual relations at the very worst time, just as you produce an egg and the consequence would be pregnancy. All this figuring is, of course, quite hypothetical", the doctor said blithely. "The rhythm method, even if faultlessly followed, generally is only 75% effective."

Mrs. Kenny was stunned by that fact. She knew 75% meant 3 out of 4. She pictured 3 empty cribs, but in the fourth, a baby, not angelic, but a baby, face contorted with anger from hunger, colic, a soiled diaper.

"Now to collect data on what constitutes the longest and the shortest days of your cycle," the good doctor continued, "keep accurate records for six months, and use this data for your calculations. Of course, I reiterate, these calculations are open to the fluctuating vagaries of your individual body."

Something immediately occurred to Mrs. Kenny, living as she did in the real world. "What should I do not to conceive while I am collecting data?" In an almost hysterical release from what she was hearing, she imagined herself in a jungle with a net on the hunt for an exotic specimen. The butterfly, violet and pink and the palest aqua, fluttered at eye level, batting her cheeks and nose and mouth at intervals with its silky wings. It was right there before her, but she could not possess it or even grasp it – it was gossamer and she was dull flesh.

Dr. Seitz was becoming impatient. He knew that this method was awash with variables, sliding up and down like so many paramecia in a Petri dish under a microscope. He, scorning churches, knew that stupidity and superstition exacted their price. He could not allow his heart to play a part in it. His detachment was icy. Getting up, he opened the door, as if to shoo out a bothersome dog, and added, "Again, Mrs. Kenny, the actual failure rate for the rhythm method, which is termed a calendar-based approach, is 25 percent. Good bye and good luck." Yes, indeed, good bye and good luck.

BENEDICTION

I, TERESA KENNY, AT TEN, WAS A DEVOUT CATHOLIC, irresistibly drawn in by the undeniable sweetness of much of Church tradition, St. Joseph sawing away purely in his carpentry shop and the Guardian Angel who warns you of a dirty bench before you sit down or tells you to look back or you'll lose your sweater. Then too there was the sublimity of church spectacle. Benediction, beautiful Benediction, its smells, its sounds, its dazzle which transported me to a world where the mysterious, and sometimes the terrifying, held sway. When my cheap acetate scarf, head covering for women was required in church, slipped down the back of my skull, and there was no way to stop it, please scarf please, it will be a sin if you slide off my hair. Tears of frustration would sting my eyes, till I could no longer read the songs of praise, though honestly, I knew by heart the words sung, "O Salutaris Hostia, Qui coel pandis ostium!" And then the blessed wafer which was God, really God, I did believe it, was lifted in its golden sunburst orb in the monstrance high, first right then left, and there wasn't a sound in the church, no one dared, except for the exquisite ringing of the hand bells, as if a bird were taught to sing soprano through a throat and beak of silver.

We all sang, even the bad boys and the bold girls, "Tatum ergo Sacramentum, Veneremur cernui," singing as if we knew what we were singing, in the incense laden smoky breath of the clanging incense thurible, swinging back and forth in the hands of the tallest, best behaved of the altar boys. We were all supposed to pin our eyes on the host and say those adoring words so that God who was in the wafer would know that he was great and be happy and would take pity on us and would not be mean to us. The stained glass windows dripped reds and cobalt blues down on our clothes, liquid color, and the plaster saints stood motionless in their purity and sanctity, though the women saints did have breasts but swathed breasts, perhaps taped down. Circling the room were the Stations of the Cross, flat sculptures illustrating the best bits of fact, how St. Veronica, lucky her, got a veil with Jesus's face on it, but where is it now, the Pope's probably got it, and a plaster picture of Simon of Cyrene helping Jesus with that heavy cross, like a good guy would. We knelt on kneelers, unpadded, but we should be glad because in the old days people knelt on the floor and were happy enough for it, they were holy then, and all around us were the stands of lit small candles like soldiers in their ranks, flickering and smoking and some guttering out, all doing their best. Then Sister Raphaela, with her little cricket clicker, directed us to get up and file quietly out of the church though by the time we got that blast of afternoon sun-brightness in our faces, Richard Gehagen and Edward Musso were already pushing one another, and Peter Toboni, the fat boy, was pulling his underpants out of his buttocks crack, walking along.

NUNS

Sister Fidelmia	Sister Peter Claver	Sister Canis
Sister Claire	Sister Consolata	Sister Raphaela
Sister Mary Dolores	Sister Patrick	Sister Raymond
Sister Alma	Sister Consuela	Sister Stanislaus
Sister Scholastica	Sister Annetta	Sister Norbert
Sister Canisius	Sister Anunciata	Sister Rose
Sister de Chantal	Sister Thecla	Sister Blaise
Sister Damien	Sister Emydius	Sister Gloria
Sister Bernadette	Sister Cyril	Sister Benedicta
Sister Antoinette	Sister Thomas	Sister Sylvester
Sister Ursula	Sister Agnes	Sister Camillus

Sister Theresa of the Little Flower

NUNS AND THEIR HABITS

Some nuns are worthy,
Some are not.
Some lie so pure
On their white narrow cots.
Some dressed hobbled
In blinders and bibs,
Some tell howlers,
Some have no fibs.

FATHER CAPWELL

AND

THE FOURTH GRADERS

WE STOOD RESPECTFULLY FOR FATHER CAPWELL as he entered the fourth grade classroom, and in a pleasing singsong we sang out "Good morning, Father" in unison. The boys bobbed their heads and each girl, the ball of her right foot tucked behind the heel of her left, crimped the knee, dipped the body, and some of us even pulling the sides of our skirts out in a pretty flounce.

We loved Father, and our greetings, curtsies and bobs were happily done. For it was not only the slightly soiled mints that he kept in his cassock pocket and offered us from time to time on the plate of his large sweaty hand. We children knew and trusted his geniality and his total lack of malice.

He had, like many aged Irish men, resumed the look of the child that he was 75 years ago – pale blue, rheumy eyes, without lashes or eyebrows, a dribbly sort of look, moist about the lips, skin thin and rosy and a look of innocence as if all the complexities of life, baffling as they had been when he was 40 or 50, had, unresolved, sunk to the bottom of his brain, leaving him with the monosyllables of mental life. He was sweet and simple, and, without intention, he conveyed these qualities to his charges.

Before coming into the classroom, he had lingered at the worn wooden table in the rectory kitchen, a serviceable place without the slightest woman's touch, not a row of cheery rickrack rimming a shelf or a lacy hankie curtain or a bright souvenir cup from a seaside carnival, no nothing of that sort. He had sat there, over the remains of two fried eggs congealing thickly on his plate, and opened his cherished *Commentry on the Catholic Catechism*, covered in a cut-up brown paper bag. He read the small passage that he loved so much, silently to himself, his lips gripping every word, so as not to slur them, an affront to elocution and proper order.

> "Show particular interest and kindness to the weak and the dull and those who are neglected or ill-treated at home. Children wish to be loved, and the less love is bestowed on them at home, the more grateful they are to the priest who treats them kindly. It is very wrong to take a special interest in the smart, the rich, the beautiful. Do not fail to ask questions of the poorly talented, but only such as may be easily answered, so as to encourage them and make them more self-confident."

Now in the classroom remembering this, Father Capwell sat back and sighed and opened the button over the belly of his stretched, worn cassock. He really was a kind man, a man with the unselfconscious sweet innocence of an angel, a rather dim angel, one settled into an only minimally reflective goodness.

I listened, the fingers of one hand interlaced with the fingers of the other hand, making a cunning mound, aiming as I was for perfection, the perfect listening receptacle for the goodness that I knew my mother wanted for both of us. I fastened my gaze upon him, my attention on his words. I was not disappointed. Today I learned about St. Benedict whom the pagans tried to poison. St. Benedict, holy as he was, knew enough to make the sign of the cross over the cup and the cup broke and the wine spilt and he was saved. O holy man! What wonderful cleverness. And Father Capwell knew it to be true. He did. And there was also St. Cunegunda. Her bed was on fire. She made the sign of the cross over it, and the fire was extinguished. O wise virgin! O the wonder of it all. We all smiled broadly over the Houdinis of the Church.

But there was more. Father Capwell knew well the saintly extravaganzas, the real, true-to-life stories of Catholic martyrs where we, with him, entered the world of high drama and frequent terror. Today our pastor told us about Alberto, an Italian youth whose persecutors threatened with being boiled alive in a vat of tar, turpentine and oil if he failed to recant his allegiance to the Pope. But taking pity on him, they softened and said, if he made only the smallest renunciation, they would strangle him, as a kindness, before the boiling. He was steadfast.

"Teresa Kenny, please stand and read to the class about St. Rose of Lima."

I stood and began falteringly, but soon picked up steam with the authority of the prose.

> "Even in her childhood Rose practiced self-abnegation and self-denial. As a tiny child she

repressed her tears and moans when her thumb had to be cut off on account of injury. She always thought of our suffering Savior, who submitted to far greater pains for our sakes. She fasted three times in the week, taking nothing but water and bread, and allowed herself little more than vegetables on other days. She took but little sleep, and that on a hard bed."

What an example for me! Seeping into my bones and brain was the half-baked knowledge that sin brought disaster, pain brought relief, and that the towering mess of life was up to me to hold up. A huge burden for a small girl.

SISTER RAYMOND TAKES OVER:

SPURIOUS INFORMATION AND HELLFIRE

FATHER CAPWELL LEFT THE ROOM, relinquishing the remainder of our religion lesson to Sister Raymond. She smiled slightly, taking in air, but smile and breath faded and she exhaled wearily, puffing out her cheeks. Her migraines and arthritis, the rascally boys made wild by boredom, the requirement of rote memorization class-wide, the repetitious lessons dull even to herself on first hearing and she had heard them every year: these bedeviled the well-meaning nun. But when need be, she knew how to crack the whip, and this she did.

Quieted, we faced the oil cloth map of Mesopotamia and Asia Minor, its colors faded to a dull tan like the sands of the Middle East themselves. Sister tapped her long wooden pointer on the frayed spots and we called out, "Babylon," "Carthage," and "Constantinople," not exactly current even then.

We, fifty of us, sat at our forty desks, the smaller children, I among them, doubled up, boy with boy, girl with girl. Five desks across and eight down, with wooden bench seats and broad hinged desk tops which when lifted revealed our books, all quaintly and frugally out-of-date; some paper, not a lot, to be used economically, back and front; and our pencil and dip pen, prim on the narrow ledge along with our ink wipe cloths, stitched together at home.

We were not without the pleasures of the classroom, but ours were not so much the thrills of exploration and discovery, but instead the more meager delights. Which of us would be allowed to fill the ink wells dotting the top of every desk, or even better, to open and close the three tiered windows, thrusting the topmost panes out over the sidewalk with a hawser pole like a mariner setting a topsail? And who would be chosen to pound the erasers together after school, sending the chalk of our everyday lessons, facts about the Saints – St. Aloysius to St. Zita; Geography – Basutoland and the Belgian Congo; and Prayers – the Prayer for a Happy Death, the Prayer for the Souls of Children in Purgatory, and the Prayer for Missionaries Lost in Pagan Lands – up into the fog of the play yard.

Next came vocabulary lesson and I dipped my pen into the ink well, shaking it just a bit so that inkblots wouldn't stain my workbook. Sister loomed over us, patrolling the aisles, guarding against mischief. The threat of insolence, however mild, must always be beaten down. Each word which we copied in triplicate was one few outside our ritual knew: oblation, expiation, salutation, scapular, salve regina, resolution of amendment, de profundis and nunc dimitis, reparation, regina coeli and ejaculation, yes ejaculation. Sister might ask "How many ejaculations have you made, how many spurts of prayer like 'Jesus, Mary and Joseph have mercy on us," that's an ejaculation, everyone knows that.

These ejaculations were handy in piling up indulgences. Suppose you had an uncle and he missed Sunday Mass because he was feeling sick. My uncle did do that, but that was because he drank a lot on Saturday night, but drinking was ok because there was no commandment against that. Now an indulgence was something I could earn for him to get him out of purgatory, the temporary hell designed for sins less important than the real mortal sins of murder or eating meat on Friday. So I could repeat, over and over again, "Sacred Heart of Jesus, have mercy on us," and it would be getting, this is important to know, I must write this down, seven years and five quarantines for each recitation, and I could stack them up in my uncle's account, so that after he died, he could get out of purgatory sooner. For my uncle, that is. Or maybe my mother.

Then there was the business of Nihil Obstat ("nothing hinders") and the Imprimatur ("let it be printed"), permissions found in the front of a book and issued by a priest like Xavier Flannery, Pastor of Precious Blood Parish, Boise, Idaho, 1914, which told us that we could read the book because, without that, we'd have to read a book to find out what was inside it, and, if we did, and it was a bad book, well, harm's done, and what a pickle we'd be in. That was the trouble with books.

Every late morning, before pre-lunch restlessness really set in, we turned to our *Baltimore Catechism*. Upon Sister's order fifty of these little green books, shabby from wear, were removed from our wooden desks and slapped down on the lid tops. These tracts were the darlings of priests and nuns, for they contained the 499 questions and answers that would fortify us for the pious life, that would instill within us the correct formulas that would put an end to all independent thought. Automatic answers, word for word, well designed and well done.

"Who made you? God made me. Why did God make you? God made me to love Him and serve Him in this world and be happy with Him in the next." So far, so good. Sweet simplicity, calming certitude. These questions and answers wrote themselves upon our minds like music. Had the Catechisms stopped there on that note all would have been well. But the Catechisms went on, travelling down dark paths all too often, carving our world of behavior into temptation, traps, missteps, blunders, sin and, finally, punishment.

Sister Raymond turned to her charges. "Today we will continue our preparation for your first confession. We have already studied the first five commandments. Now, Denise, what is the Sixth Commandment?"

Denise Bonier, very good at memorization, answered, "Thou shalt not commit adultery."

Sister glossed over the definition involved, preferring a hazy vagueness about terms.

"Get out your workbook and go directly to the Problems and Exercises and write an answer to Number Four," she instructed.

> #4. Leon and Fulvia frequently go the local picture show. Leon tells his mother that they will see the same movie that is shown at the children's matinee. This is not true. Leon insists that he and Fulvia sit in the last row although Fulvia, being a pure girl, wishes to sit closer to the screen. What are their near occasions of sin? Are they mortal sins? Must Leon and Fulvia confess them before going to Holy Communion?"

This problem flummoxed me. First of all, I had never known a girl named Fulvia. I tried to picture her. What was she wearing? A white blouse with a Peter Pan collar buttoned under her chin and a pleated plaid skirt? Did she have on her big sister's pearls? Had she that morning set her hair with bobby pins to make it curly and knelt over the heater vent to dry it? Questions of female haberdashery consumed me. And how old was Leon? The only Leon I knew was Mr. Leon Tortaloonas, a stumpy neighbor man with a head of hair like a rough-shingled shed roof and a moustache to match. He often emitted what we children politely called "air poops" as he walked along. I started to laugh. Sister frowned at me. I stopped.

But back to business. I tried to imagine Mr. Tortaloonas and Fulvia watching a movie together. I pictured them there in the dark, the light and shadow of the projector playing on and off their faces, their bodies as rigid as the downtown tobacco shop Indian statue, except when Leon reached up to scratch his moustache which must have gotten itchy, or Fulvia made sure that her sister's necklace was still on her neck. Perhaps they had already seen the matinee or maybe they didn't like the Three Stooges, I knew I didn't, all that poking in the eye and annoying jabbing. Now, as far as the back row was concerned, maybe Mr. Tortaloonas couldn't see up close: he did wear thick glasses. Or, perhaps, and here there was a dark thought: perhaps the movie was a C movie, condemned by the Legion of Decency, and warned against by the bishops and parish priests. A movie shuddered over by the parishioners since it was, after all, the only threat to purity invented in this century – close dancing and necking probably being done by Romans in their togas. Was Fulvia sitting there with her eyes clamped shut? Had Leon taken off his glasses for the sake of his immortal soul? C movies were that powerful. This was a tough one. Sister Raymond called time. I had written not a thing.

Sister was once again talking to us. "Skip two lines from your answer and be ready to take dictation. Write as I read. As I have told you before, dictation is especially important to you girls – it will be useful in your working lives as stenographers. Ready, begin. Question #387. What are the chief dangers to the virtue of chastity? The chief obstacles to chastity are idleness; sinful curiosity; bad companions; drinking; immodest dress; unseemly touches of the body, yours or others; dangerous books; occasions of sin such as after-school creameries and bus stop shelters; and certain card games, plays and motion pictures. We must be constantly on guard lest we fall into degrading sin. Very helpful is a special devotion to the Blessed Virgin."

The papers were collected and Sister turned once again to the oft repeated distinction between venial sins and mortal sins, our individual souls represented in the Catechism by three pictures of milk bottles, the first one white unsullied by sin, the second only slightly grey with venial sin – talking back or telling a fib, and the last bottle black with the stain of deadly mortal sin – missing Sunday Mass for example. The mortal ones would land us in hell, and the longest life was but a drop in the oceans and oceans of time of a wrathful God and so we should be careful and on and on and on. Oh, oh, I will never commit adultery again. If ever I did. I promise. We fourth graders were thus led away from the sweet innocence of a kind, caring God to a place of inward looking, soul searching, self-blaming spirituality, all conscience and confession. I bit my lip, trying to understand. The *Baltimore Catechism* promised answers to life's disorder, things were supposed to be tidied up in those 499 queries, but my life, and my mother's and father's lives, remained for me unsettling. I dearly wanted the pages of the *Catechism* to be pasted over the pages of my life to cover them, but they did not make it to the margins, and my real life—my mother's unhappiness and my father's moodiness—was still alarmingly there before me.

THE ANGELUS:

SCHOOLYARD PRAYER AT NOON

THE DOOR TO THE KITCHEN WAS CLOSED THE NEXT MORNING, but I could still hear my mother and father fighting. Their words flung back and forth like knives. I opened the door and went in, but they didn't stop.

"Father Capwell let me borrow this book. Please read it, Henry, please."

I could see the cover. It read, *Pathway to a Happy, Holy Catholic Marriage*.

"Father said it would tell us how God wants us to conceive and have children," Mom pleaded.

Dad swatted at it and yelled at her, "Get that tripe away from me." Ah, that was it. It was a cookbook. I knew Dad hated tripe.

Mom turned and abruptly ran out of the room.

Dad said roughly to me, "Stop your gawping, big ears, and eat your mush." But I had heard. The part about tripe, a big clue, and the part about babies, Dad didn't seem to like them any more than tripe, and that mystery word, "conceive." It seemed to me that I had heard it before – like "conduct," which along with "application" and "deportment" was on the bottom of my report card. No, it was something else, not "congratulations," but maybe "conceit," like being stuck up on yourself, or maybe it was a holy word, a secret word.

Later that day I stood in the schoolyard between Regina Jennings and Joseph Lawler in one of our geometrically perfect multiple parallel lines. It was almost noon, and the church bells were soon to ring. The sea gulls were wheeling low and high over our heads and the nuns were crisp in their habits, black heavy wool serge with white starched bibs and sail-like cornices over their foreheads, more removed in dress from humanity than even the priests. The nuns stood still, as an example to us, holding the hand bells in their right hands, the bell tongues motionless in their left, till the stroke of twelve, displaying their fastidious self-control and self-denial. We also were to stand still, breath held, and on the first toll of the church bell, each hand bell would join in a single peal, our heads would bow and three hundred children would say as one: "The angel of the Lord appeared unto Mary and she conceived of the Holy Ghost."

There it was, that word "conceive," still mystifying, something to do with the Holy Ghost, whoever that was, someone I had heard of all my life, like a black clad neighbor who only left his house by dark of night, and who never needed groceries. That was the Holy Ghost, and what did he do to Mary, there was that word again, "conceive."

That thought put aside, I stood swallowed up by ritual, as such ritualized spectacles have been designed to do down through the ages. An extraordinary happening, done ordinarily. Our black and white uniforms mimicking the nuns' black and white, mimicking the seagull's white, the black asphalt of the schoolyard, the white stuccoed glare of the church, and the singly standing, here and there, white ceramic drinking fountains, under the vast white glare of the overcast San Francisco day, not kind enough to be sunny, not wet enough to be real fog. "The Word became flesh and dwelt among us." Some of us had individually trailed away in attention and voice, but we as a body didn't fade to any extent, many feeling the obligation to carry more than their share of the vocal load. The girls in their white middy blouses with scarves tied over their chests, no lower than an inch below the collarbone. And the boys, sweaty and farty, in black and white check corduroy pants with a proper man's tie, soiled with scores of school lunches, over a white shirt. Standing, until the Angelus prayer was finished, and we children, our lunchtime exuberance dispelled, were marched back in caterpillar lines to our classrooms, our days replete with formula, devoid of inquiry.

BLOODY DAYS

THE DAYS OF THE SCHOOL YEAR RIFFLED BY, marked only by the minor feast days, The Feast of the Conversion of Saint Paul, struck off his horse by lightning on the way to Damascus, an important historical event, and Saint Blaise Day, honoring the saint who was scourged, torn with hooks and finally beheaded, but who can cure sore throats. Today, as most days, I sat in the schoolyard by myself and ate my sandwich, a thin smear of peanut butter on stale bread, and took a few bites out of a soft apple before I threw it away. As the hands on the school clock moved slowly toward our 3:10 dismissal, I grew silent and inward. Here in the classroom an order had been imposed, a clear regimenting however misguided, but that was not the case at 3618 28th Avenue. A gloom settled on me: I, feeling hollow inside, looked out the window and was shocked when Sister, interrupting my reverie, called my name for an arithmetic sum. I knew that at home dirty clothes were piled up on bedroom floors, that kitchen drawers hung open and the garbage can overflowed with trash, and that a sock had been tied around the bathroom faucet to muffle the dripping. And, the most upsetting of all, that Mom was always weepy and Dad, very cross. I dreaded going home.

Leaving school I walked home absentmindedly past all the avenues and streets set in a perpendicular pattern, the houses hinged together like stamps on a postage sheet. On the west wind came the sad moan of the foghorn and the roar of the lions in the new Zoo. But when I reached our house, things looked changed. Windows that had been sealed for years against the fog had been thrown open, the casements swung out, the double-hungs lifted up. The glass, as always, was dirty from street grit and blown sand and sea moisture. I ran up the stairs, through the front door and found my sister on her hands and knees, sinking a bristle brush into a pail of soapy water and out again, scrubbing, scrubbing the worn rug.

"What's the matter, Virgie? What are you doing, Virgie?" Anything out of the ordinary alarmed me.

"Mr. McGrew's coming tomorrow to pick up the rent money. I've got to clean this blood up or we'll be kicked out of this place."

"But where'd the blood come from? What happened? Where's dad? Where's mom? Where's Freddy? What happened?" I badgered her.

"Mom's had a miscarriage. Dad took her to the hospital," Virgie muttered, head down, still scrubbing.

Miscarriage? I looked at Virgie puzzled. Had I heard that word before? I didn't know. But it sounded bad. I stabbed at understanding. "Did someone steal Freddy's baby carriage? What are we going to do? How are we going to wheel him around?" I began to whimper and then to cry, indulging myself as my sister, only a year older, could not allow herself.

"Shut up," Virgie screamed at me. "Just shut up. Don't you know anything? You're so stupid."

"Where's mom? Where's dad?" My wailing grew. Virgie flew at me and grabbing the hoop handle of the metal pail, swung it around, sloshing the dirty water out in a half arc, its cruel edge hitting me in the face.

"I hate him. I hate her. And I hate you," she screamed.

And then almost immediately, seeing clots of blood spew out of my mouth and red streams pour from my nose, she grabbed me, and wrapping me in her arms, my blood imprinting on her cheek and hair, cried, " I'm sorry, Terry. I'm sorry."

It was all over in three minutes. Virgie wiped my face, my bloody nose and my blood smeared cheeks and chin, and tenderly applied a bandage. We refilled the pail, and together we knelt to scrub the carpet clean of blood, my mother's and mine.

####

On a day a week later after the other children and I had gone home, Sister Antoinette, my new teacher, was alone in the classroom. She loved that time of day, the rare afternoon sun glazing the rough pebbly plaster walls with an apricot glaze and everything, the ornamental holy water fount hanging by a nail near the door and even the rotary pencil sharpener, handle at the ready, all looking a little less ordinary and a little more special. Sister Antoinette was a tall, good-looking woman with a natural poise which she worked on, bringing it to a fine point. When people asked her if she were Scandinavian, she was secretly pleased, hoping it was an oblique comparison to Ingrid Bergman. She had chosen her order of nuns, certainly because of their works of mercy, but also, as she knew in her heart of hearts, because they had the best habit, with an angel-wing headpiece. Then too her order allowed the sisters to choose their own names – Antoinette, now that had a ring to it. How dismal to be called Sister Silas or Sister Egbert your whole life.

Here in her classroom Sister Antoinette could swan around, and, with carefully cultivated elegance, pick things up with a graceful swoop, pinky finger curled. Here she could pivot, hands held chest high, in an elegant twirl, as she felt her long skirt entitled her to. And here she could declaim to herself alone, the poems which showed off to good effect, her round vowel sounds, also carefully cultivated, in a high fluty voice, not the one she had been born with.

> "Behind him lay the Great Azores,
>
> Behind the Gates of Hercules;
>
> Before him not the ghost of shores;
>
> Before him only shoreless seas."

The tribute to Columbus. Wonderful. And thrilling even to herself.

Sister Antoinette was by nature a kind and generous person. For after all, she lived for her pupils. Her only relative was her brother Joe who came once a month on a Muni bus from Butchertown to visit her, and who, infuriatingly, persisted in calling her "Peg." The last time he had come, she had corrected him, and, with all tact, had incorporated a small French lesson, saying, "My name, brother, is Antoinette, please pronounced, 'An-twa-net,'" When she had turned away to switch on the lights, with a fetching dip of her headpiece, he had growled under his breath, "Putting on airs, showy cow." Of course, she pretended not to hear.

She did feel it was her mission to impart her more refined feelings to the sons and daughters of plasterers and insurance agents. When she found a child with a receptive soul, she was delighted, and she had found one in me. I adored Sister Antoinette. Earlier that afternoon in entering the classroom she had, quickly, so the other children wouldn't see, passed her hand over the top of my head and smiled sweetly down on me. I knew the secret language of special distinction. But now on to the poetry lesson. I knew what was coming: "The Highwayman" by Alfred Noyes, a perennial in Catholic classrooms.

> "The wind was a torrent of darkness among the gusty trees
>
> The moon was a ghostly galleon tossed upon cloudy seas,
>
> The road was a ribbon of moonlight over the purple moor,
>
> And the highwayman came riding
>
> Riding – riding –
>
> The highwayman came riding, up to the old inn door."

The other children sat slumped at their small desks, their hands holding up their heads, leaning on their elbows, nodding after lunch in the stuffy air of the classroom. But Sister Antoinette and I thrilled to the pounding hoof beats of the Highwayman's horse. We saw him in his cocked hat, the lace at the throat of his coat of claret velvet, and we waited for him with Bess, the landlord's daughter, the landlord's black-eyed daughter. When he came, we galloped with him into the dark night, silky with cold, Sister Antoinette clasping herself to his manly body and I, wrapping my little girl arms around Sister's slim waist, galloping, galloping, galloping over the purple moor. The highway man didn't need Bess, the landlord's daughter. He had us, Sister Antoinette and me.

But on this day Sister Antoinette arranged herself artfully behind her desk waiting for my mother, Ann Kenny. When I had turned up in school one week before with a bandaged face, Sister, because she had taken me under her wing, had phoned my mother asking for a meeting. My mother entered, distracted, in mismatched clothes, hair insufficiently combed. The nun graciously motioned her to a low piano stool before her, there to answer a few tactfully put questions.

"When I asked your Teresa one week ago how her face happened to be bandaged, she said that there was an accident involving a carriage, that she had fallen down stairs, carrying her little brother's buggy, and fallen on her nose. Is this what happened?"

Searching for the correct answer, Mrs. Kenny said in a careful voice, "Yes, it was an accident. My daughter hurt herself."

Trying to put Mrs. Kenny at her ease, Sister continued, "And she was upset. Everyone in the family must have been upset?"

Mrs. Kenny stared at the nun, astonished that a member of the sisterhood, bowed down as they all were with the responsibilities of holy days and fast days and saints days, with when to abstain from meat, the selling of raffle tickets, the crowning of the May Queen, and the oral tests in Latin for the altar boys, that anyone in that position of responsibility would have the time to ask about, to care about her child's feelings and maybe even her own. Sensing the nun's compassion, she blurted out, "And I've been having female problems."

"Well, all we ladies have our challenges in life," answered Sister.

"No, Sister, I mean female, female problems." And she lowered her voice to a whisper, "I'm not regular, you see. I don't know what to do. I'm so upset. All the time. It's like I don't know where to turn." Mrs. Kenny had really let her guard down.

Sister Antoinette seized on the last sentence. Better to focus on the solution, on advice, without focusing on the problem. Much tidier in the long run. She rose and extracted a book from the slimly furnished bookcase behind her. She had long prided herself in knowing the works of Catholic thinkers, liberating as they were.

"Now for problems of the spirit, I always count on this author, a Cistercian monk. He has such a poetic approach to worries." This author from the well-ordered simplicity of his monastic cell dispensed wisdom in the most exquisite, dreamily abstracted prose.

Sister read, mindful of her elevated vocal register and her crisp "ings," and consonant stops.

> "Like the oak tree I am at peace when I am without sin. Those who are with God feel immense peace, a harmony with the Divine, which those who are sinning do not feel. The innocent are like the stream flowing by my window, clear, innocent and full of purpose."

Mrs. Kenny listened and thought of this fine monk, sleeping on clean sheets, with no husband and his needs, no crying baby with foul diapers to wash, no children needing to be fed or burnt pots to scour, no fat to be skimmed off the soup or dishes piled in the sink. Him, she thought, with nothing to do but stare at the crucifix on the wall and call that prayer. In a rare and fleeting moment of clarity, she thought, "What a jerk."

But that moment of brave assertion was ripped away as Sister Antoinette continued, "The holy are smiled upon by God. They live in peace. The wicked are tormented." Do you see, Mrs. Kenny?"

"Does that mean that God doesn't like me?" asked the small woman.

Here Sister Antoinette was uncomfortable. What had seemed like poetic wisdom now seemed difficult. "Only our hearts can tell, Mrs. Kenny, our hearts," snatching nonsense out of clean air. Tears squeezed out of Mrs. Kenny's eyes. She blotted them away without Sister noticing, and sat there with a bright smile pasted on her face.

The nun turned to her again. "There, I can see that cheered you up considerably. Please take this book and keep it as long as you wish. No, take this book and make it your own." Sister Antoinette had almost run out of words, speechless at her own generosity. She continued. "There's something else. Here's a holy card with a prayer that I'm told is very powerful:

> Devotion to the Drops of Blood Lost by our Lord Jesus Christ on His Way to Calvary, which will be upon your death as if you had shed all your blood for the Holy Faith. It is efficacious to reflect on the blood of Jesus spilt for our sake."

Mrs. Kenny sat bewildered. She had heard from early childhood that Jesus shed His Blood for us, but she had never, to be honest, figured it out. In her heart of hearts, she knew that she would never ask another person to hurt himself for her – and certainly since He was God, he could think of a better way, couldn't He? In her head swam all the choruses of medieval thought she had heard. Was this the only help to be offered? Did it all boil down to blame for her, blame, reproach and a frowning God?

Sister Antoinette had risen and was heading for the door. So many things to do. The May Procession, the Latin tests.

As she passed, Mrs. Kenny extended her hand, certainly for a good-bye, but mostly for comfort. Pretending not to see, Sister Antoinette brushed on by, saying in the cheeriest of voices, "Goodbye and God bless." It was a tremendous refusal of kindness that would, as events played themselves out, cause that frail hand wavering in mid-air to haunt the good nun forever.

AT THE BEACH

MY MOTHER LEANED AGAINST THE BACK BEDROOM WINDOW SILL, and stretched out to grab the clothes line that bisected into equal triangles the sandy yard way below. She was a small, now wiry woman, her youthful fleshiness worn away by labor. Stooping through the open window, she retrieved a wooden clothespin from its canvas bag, attached an item of the wet wash, and then gave a mighty yank of the pulley line heavy with sodden clothes. Rhythmically she worked: stoop, reach, pin, yank; stoop, reach, pin, yank. And each time my heart jumped up as her heels left the floor and settled, left the floor and settled. I loved her so.

Our underwear hung on the line, but my mother's brassieres no longer flapped in the wind or sagged in the fog. No, the brassieres had been replaced by formless, dingy white undershirts. My mother would be a good Catholic woman, modest and pure. She would show Father Capwell. She would show Sister Antoinette. And this modesty extended to us. Virgie and I could no longer wear bathing suits to Ocean Beach where bands of sailors home from the war, and bus drivers on their day off could ogle us. Virgie didn't mind. She had found in our house's disorder a pair of shorts and a red bandana which she could wrap chastely around her neck and torso. She pranced around, sticking her bottom in one direction, then another, singing a made-up singsong. She would abbreviate the outfit later.

Today Mrs. Miller and Mrs. Lupo had asked us to go along to the beach with their children. My mother agreed, but insisted that the group should not walk north along the sand to Playland, with its "Shoot the Chutes" splashy thrill ride and the "Big Dipper," the rickety wooden roller coaster, framed, it seemed, on poles and ladder parts. Not to the Fun House whose entrance was guarded by the enormous 7 foot mannequin of Laughing Sal, rocking back and forth on her heels, thrashing her arms, to every timid child the spectre of her scariest great aunt, erratically hysterical, even berserk, perhaps with a kitchen knife hidden up under her apron. No, not there. No, not to the Fun House with the mirror maze and the record-like spinning disc that would, revolving faster and faster, send us sliding off. And especially not along the corridors with the holes in the floor that would, at the flick of a switch from the porky man in the booth, a cigar clenched in his teeth, send a squirt of air up, inflating a lady's skirt and billowing it up over her head. Everyone, especially the men, enjoyed that though the women made a big show of saying it was common. No, we could not go there.

"You will not wear your bathing suit. You will not. You will not," my mother yelled as she halfheartedly smacked my bottom with her slipper.

It was not that I wanted to wear my own suit, but I would not wear the ancient bathing costume that my mother had found in her cedar chest. Aunt Una had worn it in the swimming tank at the Pan-Pacific Exposition in the Marina in 1915, frilly ruffles at the shoulders and pantaloons almost to the knee. Was mommy crazy? In a rare and frantic defiance, I escaped her grasp and plunged under her bed. Mrs. Miller's voice at the front door cut through the house and my mother and Virgie, distracted, abruptly left me there alone, almost forgotten.

Under the bed I slept in the dusty heat of the unusual sunny day. A quarreling woke me as my father and mother moved down the hall toward me.

"You didn't care if I had another baby! You just wanted another child to make sure you weren't drafted!"

"That's a lie. I wanted to be drafted. You've no idea how an able-bodied man like me out of uniform, was looked at, sneered at – by everyone – 'draft dodger,' is what everyone thought if you weren't blind or on crutches. That's bullshit."

"Don't you curse at me, Henry Kenny. I can't bear to get pregnant again. Oh, Henry darling, I just can't do it." My mother was sobbing now.

"You don't have to, Ann Mary. There are ways, sweetheart."

"But then bad things will happen to us all – and I'll go to hell."

"That's superstition and nonsense," my father roared. "Why do you listen to them? Why?"

I heard his steps as my father, without waiting for an answer, strode down the hall. The front door slammed.

My mother crossed the room and flopped down on the bed crying. The exposed wire mattress coils bore down on me, pressing lightly into my body. There I lay, among the odd shoes and cast-off socks, a broken umbrella and a chamber pot, its dimpled enamel surface speckled black and white. It had been used the night before – I could smell it. Soon after, her sobs turned into a soft, rhythmic breathing, and I, in my private prison, also slept.

Several hours passed. Voices again woke me. Peeking out from under the bed, I saw the small room's single window, still covered with a heavy air-raid shade, seeming to glow in the heat, black in the middle with a sickly florescent glow around the edges. The door opened and light from the hallway spilled into the room.

"Mom, Mom, guess what happened?" Virgie shouted. My mother half rose, swinging her legs over the side of the bed, unpinning me. I rolled over on my side. Before me was a thicket of legs, my mother's legs, blue veins prominent, not hairless, and my sister's legs and her friend's legs, skinny and powdered lightly with sand, like sugar donuts. And all the toes, thirty in all, the girls' toes never still, rubbing fretfully the grit from ankles and insteps. My mother's toes, stubby and swollen, splayed out, hiding in the drape of her robe. Their voices went on. My sister's and her friend's, outraged, yet gleeful, in the telling of a story, an overhearing of an adult confidence, which they knew would be staggering for my mother. But they didn't care. I nudged closer to the edge of the mattress and looked up.

"We pretended to play in the sand and we kept moving," and here Virgie roared with laughter, "closer and closer to where they were."

"And then," Annette yelled, daring to interrupt Virgie, "they didn't even know we could hear them. Mrs. Miller kept saying that you were not right in the head. That just because the Pope said to, you keep getting purgnant. She says you're crazy."

"She can't have said that. She's my friend, you know who your friends are," my mother moaned.

"Well, she did say that, I'm sorry," but you could tell from her smarty pants voice that Virgie wasn't sorry at all and then the girls, for the fun of it, repeated what they had said, and when they were through, they repeated it again.

"Stop it, stop it," I had to stop them. With that I struggled to get up and out from under the bed, and my knee hit the chamber pot, sending it scudding and tipping, splashing my face and my mother's feet. Virgie roared with laughter, and Annette, taking her cue, joined in.

HAPPY VALENTINE'S DAY

VIRGIE WAS HACKING AWAY IN HER PHLEGM-SODDEN BED. Since we had no money for life's luxuries like paper tissue, she blew her nose on the gray sheets, making flower-like clumps of mucous here and there. My mother blamed herself for Virgies's cold, faulting herself unmercifully for allowing her daughter to go to the beach with Mrs. Miller. Of course Virgie had waded in the waves, something my mother would never have allowed – the undertow at Ocean Beach being as strong and unrelenting and mindless as my mother's self-reproach. Everyone knew that the water there should never be trusted beyond the toes, let alone knees and hips. And then Virgie's clothes had become wet and clammy and she had worn them all day. My mother almost sobbed in anguish, while Virgie lay back on her pillow, bored by my mother's antics, paying her little mind, frowning and trying to listen to the radio crackling out her favorite daytime soap opera, Portia Faces Life. The room was mayhem, Portia and her suitor Alphonso avowing their love, Freddy crying, my mother moaning, and I begging for a bag in which to carry home the Valentine cards.

"Valentine cards! Shut up everyone. Get mine from Sister Stanislaus, Terry. Every single one of them," Virgie ordered.

My father, standing near the front door, had an order for me too. "Take care of your mother. She's not feeling well today." What that meant I knew without explanation. Take care and come home directly after school. Take care and not let her out of the house. Take care and, if she talks to anyone, take her elbow and steer her home. I knew his urgency.

At school Sister Stanislaus looked down her bent nose at me when I tried to collect Virgie's Valentines. She was full of frowns and displeasure and her patience was notoriously razor-edged. A wrong glance could result in a violent harangue. I kept my face slack, undemanding, my chin tucked down, head obsequiously bowed. Virgie Kenny's Valentines. I myself had gotten only three – one from Sister Antoinette who gave a card to everyone, one from Joan Gray, a colorless girl whose mother seemed only to send her shadow to school, and one unsigned but bearing in tiny letters stuck into the fold, "You stink." But not so for Virgie, not Virgie. Children, I knew even then, cotton up to power like everyone else.

So when Sister Stanislaus, a nun of uncertain temper, flung open her desk drawer, I saw an enormous sloppy pile of Valentines. All for Virgie. And beyond that, in the back of the drawer, were a full dozen cupcakes, baked by a class mother for the children, a thick layer of heavy pure sugar frosting, sprinkled with sparkly crimson beads. This was excessive confiscation, especially for a nun, a Bride of Christ. I peeked a glance up at Sister Stanislaus's face, but her thin cheeks gave no blush away. She scooped up the Valentines, pushed them at my chest, and told me to leave.

To take them home to a querulous Virgie, another female of uncertain temper, this was the task of the day. The wind gusted strongly up the street from the ocean, and some of the Valentines that were desperately clutched to my chest broke loose, fluttered to the sidewalk and then turned end after end, scudding up the street, each stiff corner making its crisp papery sound. When the rain started to fall the Valentines, all chicks and birdies and ponies, congealed and the redness of the hearts and roses and "I love yous" imprinted themselves on my white middy front, staining me with their ink. Tears ran, from wind and rain and my frustration, and I with an open palm smeared the red print across my cheeks.

SHE'S GONE

TRAILING VALENTINES, I BURST INTO THE NEAR EMPTY HOUSE. Aside from the sleeping Virgie, there was no one there – my mother was gone. I ran down to the business street, where the clanging streetcars worked their way up and down the slope to the ocean and parked autos sparsely lined the curb. The windows of the small storefronts, ranging a few blocks east and west, reflected, now that the rain had stopped, the now blinding white overcast sky. Inside the merchandise lay, undusted on cluttered shelves, most items pre-war, of dubious use to anyone. I ran frantically in and out of the stores. Into Edna's Fashions, Edna, her prime also pre-war, arranging shallow boxes of ladies' slips and corsets and cotton hose, seamed of course. My mother wasn't there. Into Laidley's Dry Goods, mops and pails and nails and mousetraps. She wasn't there. Into Hildebrand's Breakfast Spot, a saltine cracker in every salt shaker and unlimited catsup with every order. Not there. Past the two taverns, the Catholic one, the H and H, Herlihy and Hughes, at one end and at the other, The Whippoorwill, my father's favorite. The whiskey smell flooding out their open doors stung my nostrils. A quick glance into their dark tunnel-like interiors told me what I already knew – she wouldn't be there. Into Bubble's School Store, Bubbles with her powdered face and permed white curls, a rouged dot on each cheek, was arranging comic books on a counter piled with tablets and hard candy sweets. "She not here, Teresa dear. Try Solari's Market."

And into Solari's Market, with tight, narrow aisles, matrons in hairnets and hats carrying hand baskets, judiciously selecting each can for that single night's dinner or the next. At the rear of the store, the splendid meat counter, white porcelain enameled display case fitted out in chromium and faced with glass. In front of the display case was my mother, framed on each side by the whitish red of veal, the bluish red of the lamb, the copper red of the beef and the speckled red and white of the hamburger. I hung back not wanting to draw the attention of the other women waiting their turn. But then I saw it, saw what they must be seeing. My mother's skirt was caught, hem tucked accidentally into the waistband, the resulting drape revealing her underpants, underpants with a blaze of red, an outrageous crimson stain, and a horrible worm-like ribbon of blood running down her leg and, plink, plink, plinking on the shiny lino floor.

I ran to her and sobbed in her ear, "There's blood on your pants, mommy."

She turned to me and her astonishing reply was, "That's good then, dear."

THE RAGMAN

"Rags, rags, tin and tallow" – that was his shout, the ragman. He sat in one of the last horse and buggy rigs in the city, the wagon behind him heaped high with unhinged metal gates, fireplace fenders, ice box doors and holed pots forgotten on the fire, everything broken. Dan sat there, clicking away with teeth and tongue, encouraging his willing old horse Harry, as they made their clomping way down the hard surfaced streets, an almost painfully slow procession, trailing a stream of children. For whenever we saw him, we abandoned our scooters and coasters, our jacks, marbles and trading cards and ran to accompany them, to yell to Dan and pet his horse.

"Give me a ride, Dan, give me a ride." All of us shouted it, but none was ever granted that wish. Till a day when Dan stopped and pointed to me.

"Come get up here with me, girl."

I wasn't the prettiest or the oldest or the youngest, but I knew why he picked me. I loved Dan and he loved me. I loved his smell when he stopped to talk to us. Not a clean smell but not a smell of body waste either. Just a smell of someone who didn't take an excessive number of baths, but used a scrape and spot-cleaning method of personal sanitation. And that done with Fels-Naptha, a hard bar smelling like an old polished shoe. I loved the way Dan and his horse matched, the old-man driver sprouting impertinent hairs from unlikely places, his nostrils, eyebrows, ears and knuckle tops, all alive with coiled silver wire-hair, and his horse, Harry, grey, balding here and tufting coarsely there.

And these rides were mine, mine alone. Virgie minded a lot, but soon the preferential treatment for which I was singled out was accepted. You didn't sniff that the Queen of England and not you was the Queen of England, did you? That was the way it was.

What a surprise one day it was to see Dan without Harry. Dan, no longer a bold spectacle, a single horse-and-man carnival, but now almost furtive, climbing the steps to each door, mumbling his request for junk, asking as it were for a hand-out, and being invariably turned away. He carried a sling across his shoulders, two canvas sacks, one to either side, twin diapers filled with meager bric-a-brac. He knocked at our door.

"Rags, old fire screens, broken knives, anything for me today, Missus?"

My mother looked at him curiously, seeing someone more pitiful than herself. Dan, seeing a momentary suspension of judgment, leaned toward her, his face inches from hers. "Harry's dead and I'm so hungry," he whispered. And he, a great grown man, began silently to cry, tears shiny stripes on his cheeks. My mother, still not dressed for the day, dabbed delicately with her bathrobe sleeve at his hairy eye sockets, his cheeks, even his snotty nose. She then without a word, only pointing her finger in the air to say wait a minute, turned and soon came back, carrying bread and a shallow bowl of soup. Dan sat down on the top step and my mother sat next to him as he ate. I leaned against the wall.

"I'm going to hell," my mother said simply.

"You are, Missus?" Dan said in surprise. "I'm not. I'm in heaven, heaven right now. Here is my food, you are my missus and here is our child."

My mother laughed as if finally seeing an answer to a complicated question. She sighed and put her head on his shoulder and rested by his side.

ANN MARY MOODY KENNY

– THE EARLY YEARS

WHO WAS THIS MRS. KENNY, MY MOTHER, TO BE SO BUFFETED ABOUT by forces that to others did little harm? She was, at least in God's eyes, not a cipher, not intended to be a pale and bloodless victim whose suffering could be casually disregarded. She was spirit and flesh, accident and intent, crippled and enlivened by life's varied circumstances, swimming like salmon spawn toward some nourishing life source. How she found the current too strong can be seen by following the happenings of her ordinary life.

Her own mother had given birth to eight children. When each new infant was delivered in the back bedroom, it was placed in an open dresser drawer until a bed could be vacated somewhere and the child now lying in the crib could be moved up. In my grandmother's house there was no concern for muddy feet; the floors were like the surface of the streets outside, sandy, gritty with the occasional sharp stone. Meals were when you could get them, and when the children stood in a line for inspection for their only communal social occasion, Sunday Mass, Grandmother used the one handkerchief to mop all their noses, telling them to blow. It was a practical, no-nonsense household.

My mother, born Ann Mary Mooney, arrived on earth in 1915 in this small house in an alley of small houses "south of the slot," that is, south of the streetcar track that ran down Market Street in San Francisco, the slot that divided laborers and their extensive families from their betters. Her father, peeling the suspenders off his sweaty work shirt, had often announced, "I have four wishes in life: to live on Dolores Street, to get a city job with the Water Department, to drive a Packard, and to be head usher at Sunday Mass at St. Patrick's Church." In the latter only had he succeeded. The always growing family had, through lack of good fortune, remained in the cramped quarters on Shipman Alley.

Here the eight children were raised. There was a oneness about the household, one bathtub; one toilet; one comb for all; one book (*The Catholic Book of Bible Stories*); one picture on the wall (Franklin Delano Roosevelt); one calendar (the Sacred Heart courtesy of Gillespie's Funeral Parlor); one overstuffed chair, reserved for Himself, Mr. Mooney; and one luxury, the table radio which called them all together in audience every night. For bedroom curtains, sheets held up by safety pins from nails in the window frame corners, and on all of the children's beds, unmatched bedcovers. Such was their life, a simplicity which was not of their choosing, lacking the kind embellishments of life: books, camera, easy chairs, pretty plates, a regular supply of clean underwear, shampoo, trips to the dentist, spare change, even fresh fruit, except for apples, and those old. Ann Mary came to want more.

She had been christened at five days to avoid the perils of Limbo, the hellish repository for the souls of unbaptized children, as taught by the Catholic Church. She was given the name Ann Mary, an awkward name on the tongue, not like the melodious Mary Ann, and her name anticipated her awkward progress through childhood.

In school she had been one to count her sums on her fingers hidden under her desk, and to get backwards the bulges on her B's and D's and the flags on her F's and E's. When presented with arithmetic tasks, Ann Mary's mind wandered off, and she made each digit a player in a cast of a play – 2 was a nice lady, but she was always being betrayed by 5, a heavily made-up villainess who wanted to be the girlfriend of 7 who walked with a limp from the war and had a thin moustache and gentle eyes. 7 was the uncle of 3 who was a little girl much like Ann Mary herself but with curly yellow hair. All these people and indeed all the numbers got together in different ways in Ann Mary's sums – who could know when 7, who was secretly in love with 2, might get together for a picnic and bring 3 along. Not to mention the possibility of 1 and 8 being invited. Math became very fascinating, but for all the wrong reasons and Ann Mary often looked up at Sister Norbert with a non-comprehending, faraway look as if she had been interrupted in the middle of a deep dream. As she had.

Ann Mary was often scolded and because she was such an easy mark, submissive and self-blaming, it was natural for the teachers, venting their general frustration, to overly chastise her. She took their remarks without protest to her heart where they smarted. Dreamy, not attractive enough to be winning, not quick enough to be amusing, always at the side of things, the choral group, class pictures, assemblies, teams, always to the back and to the side. She had few friends and spent hours outside in the alley, bouncing a ball up and down, up and down, or scraping a stick along the fence railings, slap, slap, slap, and no one noticed.

ANN MARY MOODY KENNY
– THE MIDDLE YEARS

ANN MARY LIVED AT HOME WITH HER PARENTS as young women of that era did. She was no glamour girl, but she had a kindness that sometimes expressed itself in her face in a kind of radiance. People often told her their problems, not because they thought she could solve them, but because she would understand. The postman told her how his aunt had knit him a scarf which his brother had made fun of, calling it girly. A woman she had never seen before sitting next to her on the bus told her of being jilted, quickly before she had to get off four blocks away at Fulton Street. Ann Mary came to know that there were many woes in life.

Then Ann Mary's fortune took a twist. She met my father. He had followed her home one day from her job at the Jesse Street Tearoom, and when she could no longer ignore the fact that he was trailing close behind her, she turned and said, without wit or hostility, "Are you following me, sir?" to which he answered, "If you come home with me, girl, you'll never be lost," a remark which didn't stand up to logic, but which to her seemed romantic enough. She determined to marry him.

But it was against the will of her father. He stood before her, glowering, jamming kindling into the stove's trash burner, and demanded, "Why do you want to marry him? Is it because you're 24, and no one else has ever asked you?"

"It is," Ann Mary said.

"That's a good reason," her father replied.

"Is it also because you love him?" her father further asked.

"Yes, it is," Ann Mary said.

"That's not a good reason," her father stated, living as he did in a world empty of romance. "I'll tell you right now that my friend is a better match for you," referring to his fellow hod-carrier, Mick McGinness Doyle with his three missing front teeth and his suit that had enough food on it to make you breakfast. No, she would not consent to that.

Mr. Mooney went on. "I just can tell you that I don't much like your fellow. He has a tendency to get above himself."

Ann Mary, looking beyond her father, at the grey stone sink, rarely scrubbed, the wooden drain boards, the open shelves housing little beyond jam jar glasses and chipped plates thought, "And so do I, father, so do I." She had in her heart some small desire for order and polish, perhaps even elegance, a world well-appointed. Was this asking for that much?

She threw her lot with my father. He too wanted more and thought he deserved it. He had turned down a good job, everyone said it was a good job, at a brewery and had taken classes at the Mechanics' Institute in draftsmanship. Now at Van Arsdale-Clark Fittings he sat on a high stool, poring over blueprints, number 2½ yellow Dixon Ticonderoga in one hand, slide rule in the other.

They sorted out their wedding presents together, most of the gifts ugly, all unwanted. But her Aunt Claire, however, gave Ann Mary rosary beads, real cultured pearls strung on a filigree chain, gold plate, 9 carat. She had said, perhaps thinking of her own quietly desperate marriage: you will have need of these. And Ann Mary would.

Their wedding had taken place in St. Patrick's Church under a sunny sky with all eight of the Mooney children in attendance. The ritual was secured, the arch formed by my uncles' arms passed under, my mother carried over the threshold and the marriage embarked upon according to the rules of Mother Church. This last was of the utmost importance due to the one fact that had caused my grandfather's greatest resistance to the marriage: my father was not "RC," a Roman Catholic. Henry Kenny was a Protestant Ulsterman, a dirty "Proddy," and if his airs didn't give him away, his name did – not named after a familiar saint, but an English king. Promises had been extracted from him; theirs would be a Catholic household: no artificial birth control, no infidelity, no possibility of divorce and the children would be raised as Catholics. These promises made lightheartedly would come to trouble them.

ANN MARY MOODY KENNY

– THE LATER YEARS

AFTER THEY MARRIED, ANN MARY AND HENRY KENNY MOVED only a few blocks away from her mother's house to an apartment (shared bath) over a billiard parlor with a shoeshine stand at its corner. Mr. Mooney regarded his son-in-law with scorn, for the man actually had another person shine his shoes on a regular basis. Henry would sit at the stand, elevated three feet over the sidewalk, his shoes chest high to the bootblack. During the shining, he smoked a small cheroot or smoothed his hat, stroking the felt brim or adjusting the band and the tiny feather. He seemed lost in thought. Mr. Mooney disapproved. A man should only be seen to be in contemplation in two places: in church or in a tavern over a beer. And not to overdo it in either place.

Mr. Mooney gradually came to dislike his son-in-law even more. Henry's nickname in the boxing ring, where he used to do amateur bouts, was "King Henry," a bouquet tossed him for his dignity, he would never back down. He could have done what Mr. Mooney's own sons did, show his father-in-law the proper feudal spirit, say yes but mean no, but Henry stood his ground, he didn't grovel.

"The man sits there like a king on a throne, like a constipated prig on a pot, looking down on everyone, having some poor guy attend to his shoes. I tell you he thinks he's a swell, but he's a working stiff just like me."

After two years and two children, Ann Mary began to wear down. The clink of billiard balls on the green felt below them seemed to rise through the floorboards and inhabit her dreams and she longed for the fuller life she had yearned for and been promised.

Henry proposed moving west over Twin Peaks to the Sunset district, the sandy flatlands fringing the ocean. The elder Mooneys thought little of the idea, Mr. Mooney responding to the couple's aspirations by repeating an Irish saying that, only if wedged in, fit the situation: "He'll promise you all the deer in the parkland, but you have to go get them yourself." Mrs. Mooney frowned, fearing that the constant fog in the Sunset district would prove hard on her small daughter.

Despite family opposition, Henry and Ann Mary Kenny came to live in a rented house on 28th Avenue. It was a bungalow, attached on each side, 40 houses in a row on the west side of the street with another 40 houses on the east facing them. Featureless, stucco, unadorned and unaccompanied by trees or much greenery. The fog pulled out to the ocean every morning at 11:00 and came back in at 4:00 in the afternoon, except in the summer when it stayed all day. "I've got to get the wash on the clothesline to dry" was the constant refrain in the morning, followed five hours later by "I've got to get the clothes off the line before the fog comes in." My mother seldom smiled on foggy days and it seemed always foggy in the Sunset.

And not only the fog, but the sand. The dunes, still empty of houses, were just eleven blocks away to the west: tall, sloping hills of sand that shifted every day, to us children like the Sahara. The sand, blown on the wind, carried like a thin batter in the fog, collected in store doorways and street car track slots. A soot-like layer, gritty underfoot, coated our front stairs and intruded into our lives, into our cuffs, our shoes, our jacket pockets, into the corners of the house and the bottoms of our closets. Fog, fog, and sand, sand.

Ann Mary lived in a time of drudgery for women – no chicken was eaten until its pin feathers were removed with tweezers, no cloth diapers were laundered without being first being rinsed out in the toilet, washed, and put through the wringer. No shirt was done up unless it was dipped into a pail of starch and then ironed. The broom and mop and later the carpet sweeper were used to clean the floors. No foods were prepackaged or prepared; everything was done from scratch: stews, soups, pot roasts and cakes – cooking was not a hobby or an art form, it was a necessity.

The new 4 foot high refrigerator, spiral coil mechanism on top, needed defrosting every two weeks. For that the electrical plug was pulled, the milk bottles and butter dish and occasional roast wrapped in pink butcher paper were squeezed into the kitchen sink, and, after the ice crust was carefully removed with ice pick and spatula from the tiny ice cube box inside, it was thrown on top of the foodstuffs in the sink in an effort to keep things cold. Hands were frozen purple raw, water pooled all over the linoleum, not much fun.

But it was better than the old fashioned ice box, fed not by electricity, but by the iceman, carrying up the backstairs grey slabs of ice, hanging from enormous sharp tongs, thumping against his leather apron. Yes, it was a big improvement. Still Ann Mary worked very hard and tribute should be paid her.

It was true that she had escaped the clink of the billiard balls, the sight of other people's hair in the bathtub drain, and her father's constant comments regarding the shoeshine stand and Henry's patronage of it. But five miles away from Shipman Alley might have been fifty and Ann Mary missed the Mooneys more than she had ever anticipated, and the predictable gray days lowered on her. She found that two children and then later another child were nearly all that she could handle.

For Ann Mary with her babies lived in a world of scrupulous, post-war, pre-antibiotic vigilance. When her breast milk for her infants dried up, and it soon did, the bottles and nipples and collars were washed out and placed in a huge steamer pot to sterilize in order to combat the germs that everyone now knew could kill. The pediatrician, the ladies magazines, the neighborhood chat was full of cautions about babies whose careless mothers caused them to be whisked away by germs at night in a torrent of tears and recrimination. It wore heavy on her.

She yearned for her mother, for sunshine, for competence. She had little. Her own mother had found mothering easy, relying on the will of God to decide whether or not a sick child would make it through a fever or a face blotched with spots. Ann Mary somehow could not find that confidence. Earlier photographs of her showed a small woman with the apple cheeks of health and youth, often standing with her sisters, her arms around their waists, laughing a good natured laugh, or pointing at something, or covering her mouth with a hand.

But this laughing face lengthened, thinned out and hollowed. Things became harder. The strand of her youth that she had carried forward was her Catholicism, Mass every Sunday, no meat on Friday, confession twice a month, rosary beads under the pillow. Her universe, now not inhabited by the Mooneys, was populated by the citizens of St. Cyril's Parish: the pastor, Father Capwell; the nuns of the school; and the parishioners themselves, as conforming and nosily observant as honest cops. These watchful people provided a structure as exacting as civil authority, issuing codes of behavior, moral dictums as necessarily observed as municipal law.

Ann Mary had her first miscarriage at 30. What she felt then perhaps even she didn't know. Grief, or maybe relief. What she did know about the rhythm method, or natural birth control as the Church termed it, was that it couldn't be counted on. Her mother's eight children had taught her that. She would plot out on hand lettered calendars the days of her curse, as it was called, but her cycle never seemed to correspond fully to the calculations. She counted again and again and reconsidered her sums. Henry was asked to fit his needs accordingly.

Sitting at the dressing table in her flannel gown, Ann Mary did her computations. Henry entered, almost unnoticed, and turned off the fiercely burning overhead light. He crossed the bedroom and pulling Ann Mary to her feet, took her tenderly in his arms and dropped his face into the hollow of her neck and kissed her shoulder. For a moment she was filled with reciprocal tenderness. Her Henry, her darling Henry, with the spare sinewy boxer's body, wanting her and needing her. She in her sweetness knew it was an honor. But she stiffened under her heavy nightgown and pulled away from him. "But Henry, it's not a safe time tonight."

Like dry kindling ignited by fire, he spoke angrily to her. "And who told you that – your Father Capwell, wearing a skirt like an old woman – probably hasn't had a hard-on since he was thirteen and woke up in the middle of the night in a puddle – that was it for him – never let a female get close to him, but his mother. I'm sick of your priests, girlies, all of them. What the hell does he know about us, Ann Mary, about me?"

"Oh Henry, please don't insist. You know I can't refuse you. That's a sin too. But if you say it's ok, that we can wait till next week, I won't commit a mortal sin."

"And now you want me to say that I don't want you. What kind of reasoning is that, woman? I'm sick of your Church. I'm sick of you caring more about an old man living alone in a house ten blocks away than you care about your husband. Hell, you care more about that little Italian in Rome, eating off gold plates, bowing bastards all around him, doing God knows what under sheets smelling of perfume – you care more about him!"

Ann Mary used the one defense left to her: she began to cry. Henry was unmoved and he continued to rail at her. "I've got blood in my veins, Ann Mary, blood. When I got punched in the nose I'd spurt blood. I'm a man, and you're lucky to have me and you don't even know it."

He stood there, fists clenched, looking to take on the priests, the Pope, anyone. How dear he was to her, not a tall man, but scrappy, bold, virile, a heart as big as a lion's. She wept with love for him.

He was through. He hardened his heart toward her. He didn't hit her, he didn't force himself on her. He pulled on his trousers and shirt, and slinging his jacket over his shoulder, turned and left the room and the house.

This was Ann Mary Mooney Kenny's life in San Francisco in 1946.

HOPE

MY MOTHER WAS NOT DOING WELL. My father had moved down the hall and there shared the narrow twin bed, pushed up against the wall, with Freddy. No one visited us. The house, which had never been lively, was even more quiet, a deep silence, full of shame and anxiety, filling the hall of closed doors. When my mother at last got up out of bed, she was ashen, fragile, and full of uncertainties, asking me at age ten at every juncture what to do. Do you think I should toast this bread again, or will it burn? Shall I wear a sweater, am I cold? Is this meat good, have I left it too long, do you think it smells bad? I was staggered, at sea. Part of me hated her. Why couldn't she make these judgments? She never changed out of her bathrobe now, and she seemed unwilling to bathe. My little brother became fretful and whiney and hollered angrily when I left for school.

One day though stands out distinctly from the rest. My father did not leave for work, but with determined, deliberately manufactured cheeriness, dressed Freddy and took him next door to Mrs. Klein. He then pushed my mother into the bathroom and I could hear his jollied voice booming from behind the door, "Use more soap. Here I'll fix the faucet for you. Don't mind, don't mind, I'll wipe up the water. I'll do it." My mother, dazed and moist, came out. "We're going to a special doctor. Tell your mother how good she looks," and then, without waiting, he had her out the door and into our old car.

That afternoon after school Virgie and I sat in the darkening of the living room. It was well beyond the time of expecting their return. The sky, still shone a bluish grey, but the houses across the street were black shapes, and as we sat, the sky dimmed into the same black and consumed them. Virgie crossed the room, and squeezed in beside me, into the small hollow of the overstuffed chair, and put her arms around me in the dark. The edge of my body melted into the warmth of my sister's, and she turned and pressed her moist lips on my forehead, and said, "If Dad doesn't come back, they'll put us into foster homes. I won't let them take you away. I won't let them."

There suddenly was a racket on the outside stairs and the door flew open and my father and mother burst in, turning on every light switch before them, filling the house instantly with light and noise. "We've been to the doctor and then we got your mother a haircut," Dad shouted, and my mother swirled around, elbows bent shoulder high, hands cupping her face. Her hair, now that the weight had been removed, hung loose and lovely in short curls around her ears. Dad laughed and taking her hand, spun her round and round like a top and then caught her in his arms and kissed her on her mouth and kissed her again lower on the bare notch of her neck, above her collarbone. She laughed in return and playfully batted him away with a flurry of little pats. We children laughed, but softly, stunned by the originality of their behavior. It would remain for us the highpoint of our childhood, a moment put away preciously in our memories, too fragile to review, too holy in its joy to forget.

IN A WINK

WE RODE THE STREETCAR DOWNTOWN, MY MOTHER AND I, both intent on a mission. My mother to see Dr. Shapiro once again, me to eat toffee crunch cake at Blum's Bakery. It was my birthday. Hand in hand, we walked up Powell Street to the medical building, swank and Art Deco. I sat in the lobby (no one but patients allowed in the waiting room for reasons of privacy) and looked at the murals around me, the flat, heavy faced men on the piers of the city, lifting bales and crates, checking cargo manifests, twining piles of coiled rope. I felt content, surrounded by the placid, purposeful forms. Near the door was the physicians' directory, most of the doctors' names followed proudly by their specialty, but Dr. Shapiro and a few others had none and were silent, keeping to themselves.

Facing me were the deeply embossed elevator doors, six in a row, and with punctual regularity, the red light would blink, the small bell would sound, the door would slide heavily open, and the elevator operator would pop out of his box, like a cuckoo in a clock, angling his body into the lobby, and call out "Elevator going up!" They were smartly uniformed, their double-breasted short jackets fitted snugly to the chest with ten gold buttons, and pillbox hats, secured squarely under the chin with a strap. As one operator leaned over to swing closed the heavy latch of the door, he would catch my eye and wink.

What fun. I sat there and waited for the gift of a wink. My mother strode out of one of the elevators. She seemed resolute and sure, her shoulders set squarely, living up to the challenge of her broad shoulder pads, her hat banded with a smart, striped ribbon, her smooth kid gloves all seeming to correspond to the general capability of that lobby. Everyone, everything, hats, elevator buttons punched firmly, doors slung resolutely, floors announced with authority, this was the way to live life. Face on, without hesitation, without explanation.

My mother and I left the medical building and walked down to Union Square. We were both dressed up, my mother wearing a new dress and coat, made of the same navy blue fabric, but when the coat blew open, there was revealed – the glory of it – a bright orange lining. She had remarked that Dr. Shapiro thought it an excellent choice, and telling me, my mother laughed.

In Blum's we sat at a white linen table on a slightly raised platform on the aisle near the revolving door, seeming to review people as they spun round and entered. The door's compartments, solid slabs of plate glass fitted out in luxurious golden frames, moved silently and with great weight, and emitted one or two or sometimes three people, seeming to be presented as if to royalty. My mother and I looked at one another across the table and smiled. The waiter came, decked out in formal black suiting and white shirt, with smart napery draped over his arm, and stood formally erect, ready to receive our order. My mother, taking full pleasure from a stretched-out, complete sentence, said, "I believe that I will have the chocolate éclair." My mother didn't remove her coat, but let it curl back from her shoulders, sliding down slightly and revealing the orange lining. Her hair, glossy and waved, sat like a light rosette in the middle of a bright colored circle of orange petals. We sat there in a pool of unfocused elegance, drinking in the sight of matrons in fur coats, and elderly dowagers with their attentive heirs hanging on their every word and wish, and prim aunties with their indulged, pinafored nieces, all the human apparatus of the cosseted, proper middle and upper classes.

Suddenly, the door twirled one more time and out came Mrs. Miller with her children. My mother halfway rose, nudging the table before her, and I saw the joy rising in her, like a glass being poured with water. What was she thinking at that moment? Likely – here comes my friend. She can see now that I'm all right. That I'm acceptable once again. But Mrs. Miller was busy, squiring her children down the aisle. She walked four steps towards us. She saw us. She pivoted around and, surely as a sheep dog turns its lambs, she reversed her direction, and, in a wink, she, and her children, were into the revolving door, round about and out. My mother sat motionless, her lips parted and trembling. She stood up abruptly, and, barely looking to see if I were following, left the restaurant. We took the streetcar home in silence. The next morning before school her bedroom door remained closed. My mother had returned to the land of misery.

MRS. KLEIN, MRS. KENNY AND THE ST. CYRILS MOTHERS' CLUB

MRS. KLEIN STOOD OUTSIDE HER HOUSE on a joyless street lined with bungalows, each sealed with chalky stucco, and happily watered her few geraniums. She was a woman who had learned from hard times to extract every bit of pleasure from life: at this time the beaded arc of water from her handheld sprinkler glistening in the setting sun, and the strength of her calves and the solidity of her feet on the concrete sidewalk. She, who had lived through endless Russian winters, found it difficult to leave her house without her coat and so she appeared always like some sort of immense Siberian bear, wooly and dark. That, and her heavy accent, leaden posture and hair drawn down into a braided bun set her apart from the other women on the block, Irish and Italians, all Roman Catholics. She lived as an observer, observing mostly the embattled family next door to her, the Kennys.

Mrs. Klein was also an ugly woman, who knew her share of social scorn, but she had been graced with great good fortune in her Herman, a bald lean pillar of a man who loved her unremittingly. From Herman's love she had learned the healing power of tenderness, unexpected, not required, flowing out across the universe, finding somehow its rightful target.

Mrs. Kenny and her middle child were leaving their house now. When Mrs. Klein called out to them in greeting, the little girl answered. The mother's face was very white and her mouth had been outlined in a crooked crimson color, perhaps by a shaky hand. The little girl did most of the talking for her mother, and gently held her hand, to guard her mother, in an assumption of responsibility that brought tears to Mrs. Klein's eyes, because so much was being asked of the child.

"Where are you going, dear? Ah, Mrs. Kenny, to the Mothers' Club – that's good – to talk about your children and complain about your husbands – with all the other young mothers. That's good. I did that too. And your daughter will walk with you. And then she'll go home to do her homework and go to bed early – school tomorrow, huh? And when will the meeting end? Not too late then. Go now and have a good time, my dear." Mrs. Klein, the only woman on the block who did not turn and quickly enter her garage when she saw Mrs. Kenny coming, waved them goodbye.

A few blocks away Mrs. Kenny walked alone into the basement church hall, all the chrome capped lights glaring extravagantly overhead, the room alive with the chatter of the forty or fifty women of the St. Cyril's Mothers' Club. They stood in little knots of three or four or perhaps larger groups, shoulder to shoulder, in loose closed circles. Mrs. Kenny, on entering, felt the energy and what seemed like happiness and responded with a bright smile which became more and more lopsided, sliding over her strained face as she passed by all the female bodies, all turned away from her, each as impervious as a stockade. She threaded her way across the waxed linoleum, past the rows of metal folding chairs stationed at each rectangular Formica table braced up by sturdy steel tube legs, and she found not one opening, not one shoulder twisting to welcome her in, not one smile of recognition bidding her to join them. A fortress of narrow congeniality, excluding her, directing her wordlessly to move on. She finally found refuge by sitting at one of the empty tables, her smile now dug deep in her face.

Gradually the places at the table began to be filled, but tentatively from the far end and stopping one place away from her, as if those seeking seats were doing so guardedly, fearing contamination from the small woman at the other end, who sat still hopeful for some kindness. She was but a small distance from them, yet not with them, her wobbly crimson lipstick line and wrinkled clothes and nicotine-yellowed fingers revealing her distress, and they, to be kind to them, behaved like people seeing a stranger with a crusty, red rash of undetermined nature which one might catch if one ventured too close. Better to leave her alone. Better to pretend she didn't exist.

The women's conversation fired up as they began to talk feverishly as if there were some sort of competition between the tables for animation, for sparkling cleverness. It flashed back and forth, many remarks non-sequitur.

"And I did say to my husband Edwin, 'How would I know that? You're the brains in the family, or so you've told me,'" and the heavy woman with the acutely arched eyebrows, chirruped at her own riposte.

"Oh, Maureen, you didn't, did you," said her neighbor, exclaiming at the minxishness of her portly friend, putting in play the mutually exchanged flattery that was the coin of commerce here.

"No, I do not dye my hair. What in heaven's name gave you that idea? It's just that I was sick last spring and it affected my hair color. That happens, you know. I'm doing fine now."

And one woman to illustrate her knowledge of current events informed the others, "They let a Negro into the Senate Gallery last week. He says he's a newsman and that his name is Percival Prattis."

"Percival! Well, I never! Doesn't that beat all?" replied her shocked companion.

Mrs. Kenny at several junctures had raised her head, her up-tilted mouth half articulating a timely comment, her eagerness to join in indicated by a timid raising of her eyebrows and hand, but she was invisible to them. Eventually, her elbows on the table, her arms along with the table top forming a protective triangle in front of her, she sank her face into her hands. She didn't cry. She just gave up.

Later when the women were through with their gay conversation and sugary cake, and after they had said their loving goodbyes to one another and picked up their possessions, Mrs. Kenny too got up and left. Standing in the darkness to the side of the church hall doors, off a ways so as not to be seen, Mrs. Klein waited for her. Seeing her exit after all the other women had left, as solitarily as she had entered, the old woman approached her.

"There, did you have a good time? I bet you did. I was just

telling Herm it's a nice night for a walk and so I'll go get Mrs. Kenny at her church," and as she spoke, a puff of her warm breath turned into steam in the cold air. "I'll just go get Mrs. Kenny so she'll have someone to walk home with."

She looked down at the small woman, and seeing her anguished face and guessing at the night's events, she tenderly put her large peasant hands on either side of Mrs. Kenny's head and, tenderly, like a rabbi blessing a supplicant, kissed her on the forehead. Linking her arm in my mother's, they walked home.

ANN MARY MOODY KENNY'S MENTAL BULLETIN BOARD

THESE WERE THE THINGS WRITTEN ON THE BULLETIN BOARD of Mrs. Kenny's heart – scrawled in indelible ink, not permitting erasure or amendment. All the everyday worries and all the edicts of authority held sway on her psyche– her strict Catholic girlhood and her timid nature did not allow her to follow the promptings of her heart. These things swam in her mind; they were the background noise of a troubled soul.

Infantile Paralysis, Polio Epidemic, San Francisco, Summer 1946

>Symptoms: fever, stupor, vomiting, headache, paralysis of limbs, pain, death

To tell Virgie and Teresa

>1. Don't let your bottom touch public toilet seats.

>2. Don't let your lips touch the porcelain spouts of drinking fountains.

>3. Don't go to Fleishhacker Swimming Pool.

>4. Don't get over-heated or chilled. Take off sweater, put on sweater.

5. No ice cream cones, no popsicles, no sharing of food.

6. No going to Pat's house; her mother doesn't open the windows every day: stale air.

To myself

If Virgie or Teresa or Freddy complain of sore arms or legs, wring out a towel that has been soaked in salt water, and wrap the limb from ankle to knee, or wrist to elbow, and cover tightly with blankets. Pray for the best. My mother had eight children. She only lost one.

O, Mother of God, help me!

Examination of Conscience

Pious Catholics should examine their conscience every evening at night prayers. All people, even children, should reflect upon what evil thoughts, words and acts they were guilty of during the day at home, at church, at school, or in the street. Everyone should consult the Table of Sins (*Prayerbook for Everyday*, page 59). When we are about to retire at night, if we believe that we are in the state of mortal sin, we should strive to make an act of perfect contrition and resolve to go to confession as soon as possible, for how many people, even boys and girls, retire at night in good health, and are found dead, their sin unconfessed and unforgiven, in bed in the morning.

The Act of Contrition

> O my God, I am heartily sorry for having offended Thee, and I detest all my sins, because of Thy just punishment, but most of all because they offend Thee, my God, who art all-good and deserving of all my love. I firmly resolve, with help of Thy grace, to sin no more and to avoid the near occasions of sin. Amen.

Granma Mooney's Rules for Health

> Don't sleep in a draft.
>
> For a sore throat pin a wool sock around neck.
>
> Boil handkerchiefs.
>
> Don't drink milk if you have the croup.
>
> Insert newspaper down inside your shirt front to protect against chills.
>
> Stew apples for runs, and stew prunes for blocked bowels.
>
> To cure an earache, tobacco smoke puffed into the ear, is often effective.
>
> Lingering on the toilet leads to piles.

Story of a Pure Virgin

> There was a virgin named Thecla. Her parents espoused her to a man. But the love of virginity had kindled in her heart. She ran away, but was

apprehended by Roman authority who stripped her and placed her in a public theatre. Her innocence shrouded her like a garment. Then lions were let loose upon her; they fell crouching at her feet, and licked them as in veneration. Even fire could not harm her. After many a torment she was called to Our Lord, with the double crown of virginity and martyrdom on her head.

Nice Pot Roast (Henry's Favorite)

Brown shank of beef in hot lard with lots of salt and pepper. Add pieces of parsnips, turnips, potatoes and carrots. Put in soup bones (get from Solari's Butcher). Pour in 3 glasses of water and 1 glass of Worchester Sauce. Boil for 3 hours. Take off the fire and put in cooler till fat hardens on top. Lift fat off and save for cooking later on. Take out bones. Skim top cream off of a pint milk bottle before shaking it. Mix cream with a saucer of flour. Stir broth, a little at a time, into flour, and then add to pot roast liquid. Heat once again. Very nice.

Prayer After Every Sunday Mass, 1946, Said for the Conversion of Russia

St. Michael, the Archangel, defend us in this day of battle, be our protection against the malice and snares of the devil. Rebuke him, O God, we humbly pray, and by thy divine power drive into hell Satan and the other evil spirits who wander through the world seeking the ruin of souls. Amen

Remember to Keep Private Calendar (Very Important)

Aunt Claire's Rosary Beads in Pocket

I do have need of them. Find the cross and travel down the small beads. No one need know if I keep my lips still. The Creed – all things we must believe. "Conceived of the Holy Ghost, born of the Virgin Mary, was crucified, died and was buried." On to the big loop, the Joyful Mysteries: the Annunciation. Mary was happy when the Angel Gabriel told her that she was going to have a baby, and she wasn't even married yet to Joseph, why wasn't she ashamed, I don't know, beats me. Then on to the Nativity, say Hail Mary, Hail Mary, Hail Mary, no one would give them a room, but the Magi came bearing gifts, but Mary and Joseph didn't need frankincense and myrrh, they needed a room, keep your mind on the mystery, and then the next ten beads, The Presentation of Our Lord, I don't know much about that, and the last beads, The Finding of Our Lord in the Temple, after they lost Him and He had gone back, without permission, to preach, what a scamp, He'd get a good whack from me, oh no, He was God, wasn't

He? And end with "Hail Holy Queen, Mother of Mercy, our life, our sweetness and our hope, to thee do we cry, poor banished children of Eve." Amen.

Jesus, Mary and Joseph, I give you my heart and my soul.

Jesus, Mary and Joseph, assist me in my last agony. Jesus, Mary and Joseph, may I breathe forth my soul in peace with you.

O, Mother of God, help me.

FRANK AND ANN MARY

A FEW WEEKS AFTER THE MOTHERS' CLUB MEETING, Francis Evelyn Ashcroft stood before the women of St. Cyril's Parish at their quarterly Ladies' Evening of Recollection. Ever so often the Archbishop would send Francis, his male secretary, though not a priest, to inject a little pep into the women's proceedings, to show that the Archbishop cared, and to keep the donations up. There was nothing like a man to tell the women what to do. Francis and the Archbishop were in accord on that.

The rosary had been gotten through, and the address delivered. In this Francis preferred to use the Archbishop's own words, the same little speech each time – why fiddle with inspiration – the three months interval would make it unfamiliar enough. The subject was always "GRACE:" "G" for God; "R" for rosary; "A" for attendance at Sunday Mass; "C" for Catholic; and "E" for eternity. Took a tidy 13 minutes and that was fine. Then followed the milling around him of the ladies, many of them elderly and frizzed haired, they in adoration of the Archbishop's emissary, and he, drinking it all in, he even got to call them "my dear child" like a real priest. Off they went then to the kitchen to return with red Jello poured over with cream and butter cookies (his mother had the recipe).

Francis had said his goodbyes outside when it occurred to him that he had left the Archbishop's script behind. He popped back into the parish basement hall, and, as he stood there, out from behind an old disused statue of Mary, face a bit crumbled from a fall in an earthquake, slipped a small youngish woman, really rather pretty, light curls framing her face, the wrinkles caused by constant worry hidden in the dimming light, as the janitor began to switch off the overhead lamps. She was as lovely as the Blessed Virgin, as lovely even as Loretta Young playing the Blessed Virgin. Francis was moved at some level of his being and into his mind came the melody, "You and the night and the music…" No music, but somehow this encounter struck some emotional chord.

"Can you help me?" she said.

Francis sucked in his breath and drew his shoulders back. "Yes, of course," and a little tapped strand of nobility rose in him. "Of course." The woman, wafted as it were by a small breeze, surged gently forward against his jacket, laying her cheek on his shirt front, breathing against his chest, and murmured a heartfelt, "Thank you."

An enormous sweetness came over him, an intimation of something hitherto unknown, of a possibility of tenderness beyond his experience. He touched her gingerly on her elbows, and, bending, kissed a private part, her ear, and brushed back a curl from her white neck, and yearned to cup her breast with his hand – but didn't. A moment as deeply tender, as intimate, as Francis would ever experience in his entire life. Of course he would help her. She, in her worn suit and tattered gloves, was beauty itself.

The clatter of the custodian coming down the stairs startled them and they jumped back and faced one another. Francis said, not in his own voice, but in the voice of one for whom the universe is wonderful and uncertain, "What is your name?"

She answered quickly, "Ann Mary."

"My name is Francis, no Frank. I work at the Chancery Office. Send me a note. I'll help you." My mother turned and ran up the stairs, passing the janitor on the way. She had come and gone like a dream. Frank stood there, touched in his heart and motionless.

A SIMPLE REQUEST

A MILE AWAY AT THE BEACH THE BREAKERS SLID UP THE SAND, not gloriously but monotonously, doing their duty. The houses that layered in a strict grid up away toward the east were also just doing their stolid duty, not seeking any quality beyond the ordinary, and so became as dismal as the vastness of the fogbound ocean would allow them.

But in the house next door to the Kennys sat a man in a skullcap in a heavily patterned room, formations of burgundy roses crawling across the carpet and where they met the baseboard, mutton-colored vines scaled the walls to the ceiling. And everywhere that something wasn't – between the heavy lumps of furniture, around the floor lamp on its pole and glass ashtray on its pedestal, was the smell of cabbage, up your nose, down your gullet and maybe even in your ears, cabbage on the stove now or yesterday or tomorrow.

But the tall, balding man who sat there had a soul beyond all this – a soul of clear generosity and honor. He waited for my mother, who, just now, along with his wife, Mrs. Klein, had left our house, walked down the front stairs, across the narrow rectangle of grass and up the stairs to Mr. Klein's house and through the front door.

"I'm enchanted to meet you, Mrs. Kenny, in my own house," said Mr. Klein in greeting.

He had this morning chosen to wear the better of the two identical suits he owned, the one he wore to High Holy Days, dark wool three piece, jacket, trousers, and vest, over a white shirt starched stiff. In the vest pocket he had carefully inserted his gold pocket watch, given to his grandfather by the manager of the Krakow Electric Works in recognition of good service some seventy years before. Mr. Klein had also polished his boots, first laying out sheets of newspapers and the waxy rags, and then rubbing with a kind of devotion the leather flanks and around the laces which were not threaded into buttonhole eyelets, but wrapped around posts, across the instep and around the next post and across again.

All this and the care it took to dress every morning reflected a respect, not only for himself, but for others. He was an honorable and decent man who would give his seat on the street car to any woman, the shabbiest charwoman or the most rouged tart. He carried within him a code of morality that came not from what he had been taught, but from what he himself knew: that people should not be hurt, they should be respected.

"I have great confidence, Mrs. Kenny, that we can together write a document that will explain to the elders of your church your situation and will happily resolve your problem. When they understand, how could they fail but be moved by your plight? How could they not, being people of holiness? I have every confidence. Believe me, trust me, believe in goodness, my dear. Please let me help you."

Mrs. Kenny settled deep into the overstuffed chair and felt such an air of warm expectation that left her glowing. "Oh, do you think so, Mr. Klein, do you really think so?" Her face for those moments regained the sweet innocence of earlier days.

Mr. Klein rolled his shirt sleeves up just little to protect them from ink stains and, as he did so, small tattooed numbers on his forearm were revealed. Mrs. Kenny, out of her polite discretion, made no mention, and Mr. Klein did not boast or apologize. No comments were exchanged, a credit to both.

"Please, Erna, bring me the paper we brought from St. Petersburg. For important purposes. We shall cut off the heading reading "The Helvetia Hotel" and instead write your name on it, Mrs. Kenny, and my own."

Mr. Klein stooped over the small table and began to write. He desired, with his whole heart to help his neighbor, and so his handwriting was as close to a work of art as his arthritic hands could achieve. Scrolls, loops, hanging curls, beautifully composed letter sequences and punctuation as florid as commas and periods and apostrophes have ever been.

> "To your Worship, the Excellency, the Archbishop of the worthy Catholic Church of the World."

Oh, that was a good beginning, conveying great respect. But the next words were not as easily written, given Mr. Klein's decency which was overburdened by a great delicacy. But he persevered. The words scratched off his fountain pen.

> "And as I have explained, Mrs. Kenny's situation is a difficult one. The irregularity of her menstrual cycle makes it impossible for her to do her conjugal duty to her husband without fear of issue, which

would be harmful to her health and injurious to the family's financial well being. And so it is necessary that she be relieved from this one prohibition, and be allowed the use of contraceptives, in all else being an observant, devout member of the Roman Church. With every trust in your understanding, we remain, Mrs. A. Kenny and Mr. H. Klein, scribe."

"Now," Mr. Klein said, as he pushed back from the table with a contented sigh, "that has been taken care of. Be at peace, Madame."

But Mrs. Kenny wasn't that sure. It did seem reasonable, but she suspected that there was a secret that only the Catholic Church knew, that would like a burst of air from strong lungs, blow down all the house of cards that Mr. Klein, in his careful and loving rationality, had balanced on edge. She wasn't sure at all.

ST. ZENO

MR. KLEIN HAD GIVEN ME THE LETTER. "Please take this letter, Teresa, to your school's principal and ask her to give it to the holiness, the Archbishop. It is very important to the well-being of your family. It will make all things right."

I thought about it for a minute and remembered the principal's office, with cardboard boxes around the room's perimeter overflowing with faded mimeographed copies of old grammar and mathematics exercise and examination sheets, and her desk stacked high with more of the same. The whole room smelled of something unsavory – perhaps an old bologna sandwich in a bag lunch brought by a mother for her forgetful son was wedged in there, not to be remembered until Sister Damien's departure or death. No, I could not entrust the letter to the principal. I would have to deliver it myself.

Father Capwell had mentioned once in a Sunday sermon that the Archbishop worked in the Chancery Office next door to Mission Dolores. I asked Bubbles in the school store down the street, how to get there on the streetcar. She stopped stacking the Bannister color pencils on their racks and looked at me curiously, her bright eyes enormous behind her thick spectacles. Like most adults I could trust, she didn't ask questions. "Take the L streetcar to Church Street and transfer to the J and then you can walk the rest of the way. Do you have the address,

Terry?" I had already gotten that from the telephone book. I could handle these practical matters. But I did need extra help, from on high, and so I went to Sister Antoinette. I could count on her.

But Sister Antoinette that day was, unfortunately, in the mood for questions. "The Patron Saint of letters? Perhaps you mean is there a Patron Saint of letter carriers, postmen? Is that what you want, dear?"

"Yes, yes, my uncle is a postman." I was thinking fast.

"And does he have a need for a special saint? That's a silly question – we all have a need for a special saint. But does he?"

Sister's small rambling gave me time to come up with an answer.

"He got bit by a dog."

"Oh how dreadful. What is his name?"

"George, his name is George."

"Well, I'll pray for him."

"For the dog, Sister? You'll pray for the dog?"

"No, I meant for your uncle. What is his name?"

"His name is George." Now I was totally confused, tangled in the web of my ten year old's prevarication.

"But you said that the dog's name is George. Is your uncle's name George?'

"They're both named George, Sister, but his brother isn't named George. His name is Tom."

"Oh, you have another uncle named Tom?"

"No, the dog's brother is named Tom, but he's small and never bites."

Sister looked confused and I was entirely confused. She found a way to end the conversation. "I'll look up the matter in "The Catholic Almanac" during my lunch hour and I will let you know after school. Be a good girl and eat your whole lunch. You're too thin." And she was off.

####

The day went by slowly. I had slept the night before with the letter under my pillow and now I envisioned it, where I had so carefully put it, inside my battered lunch box, never separated from me. When the school dismissal bell rang, Sister Antoinette was immediately at my side. She had, against the rules, taken a volume of *The Catholic Almanac* back to the classroom for me. She excitedly opened it to the pages devoted to Saints and slid her forefinger down the whole alphabetical list from St. Aloysius of Gonzaga, past St. Edmund of Kent and St. Martin of Tours, and then, speeding up, past St. Odo, St. Philip, and St. Polycarp, Bishop of Smyrna. Then a few inches down from St. Sebastian martyred with a hundred arrows, she stopped at St. Zeno of Antioch. Marie Curie, close on the trail of radium, couldn't have been happier.

"You see here," she said in a whisper, "St. Zeno (367AD to 417AD). Patron Saint of Letter Carriers, lived in the time of the Roman Empire. He was postal officer to Flavius Valens, Emperor, entrusted with the distribution of correspondence. Upon the death of Flavius, St. Zeno resigned his post to live as a hermit, in Asia Minor. There he lived in a cave, a meager and solitary life with no worldly chattel for comfort. He emerged only to draw water from a nearby spring and to attend Mass."

Boy, that was impressive. St. Zeno was just the guy to help me. He could fortify us, Sister Antoinette, me and Uncle George against life's onslaughts.

"Not every child cares so much about her uncle. I'm proud of you," were Sister's words as I left the classroom with the precious letter in my lunchbox, on my way to catch the streetcar to see the Bishop.

The L streetcar plunged into the darkness of the Twin Peaks Tunnel. The mirror-like reflection of the lighted car, bordered by the window frame before me, flashed by – light, then the dark of the tunnel walls, then the reflection of the lighted car again – the flash of my pale face on the window with the other few passengers, huddled, dormant, suspended in their own interior world of thoughts and worries. Black, flash reflection, black, flash reflection, ripping by wildly, like cards in a shuffled deck till in one mirror-like frame appeared a man next to me. He had an untidy grey beard and a peculiar hat on his head, like an Egyptian pyramid, and he was wearing a long purple robe. He had a kind look on his face as if his patience was a work of centuries.

I blurted out, "You're St. Zeno," and he nodded gently.

I opened the lunch box on my lap and took the letter out guardedly to show him, only him. He said, "I know. I know. Be calm, all will be well." The streetcar swayed from side to side as we hurtled on.

"Are things very different now, St. Zeno, from the fourth century, Anno Domine when you lived," I asked trying to make polite conversation, and he became very talkative, telling me about camels and wells and the various kinds of palm trees.

"People think that I wanted to go off to that cave in the rock and live there all dark and damp and solitary, but I would have much preferred a home at the oasis with a sunny exposure and a wife and four children. The problem was that my letter – written on papyrus and rolled up properly – never got to Julia asking her to marry me. A real mess up. And that was how I decided to go into the saint business. I became the patron saint of letter carriers – they need me, young lady."

The L car emerged onto Market Street, and, as it made its rattling way down, the car filled up and two old ladies stood in the aisle. St. Zeno and I, of course, got up to give them our seats. When the ladies hesitated to take them from us, I said, "That's all right. We don't mind standing." The company of a saint brings out the best in you.

We got off at Church Street and transferred to the J for a few blocks and then walked.

St. Zeno kept darting into small stores, saying, "I'll just have a look." He came back with two packs of Double Bubble gum, a tin whirly gig spinning toy, and several picture postcards. "They are a fine representation of life here and now, and show the robustness of your people," he said, waving a photo of Betty Grable in a bathing suit. "You go on now. I think I'll stay and peruse them further. I'm sure you can find your way. Keep smiling, even if you don't feel like it. A smile will light your way. And now this – " he said slowly, "the best place for a letter is with other important letters." He touched me lightly on the head and was gone.

I PUSHED OPEN THE HEAVY DOOR OF THE CHANCERY OFFICE AND STEPPED INSIDE. It was the kind of place that the outside weather never touched – sleet, heat, wind and rain could not here make an impression – it was sealed away by attitude and architecture. There in a small anteroom, cheerless and impersonal, on small tables near hard chairs, were stacked magazines, "St. Florian's Messenger," "The Western Catholic", and curiously, "The St. Francis Newsletter for Those in Service to Our Blessed Redeemer Through the Animal Kingdom." All for the faithful's edification, and, improbable as it seemed, enjoyment.

 A narrow hallway, dimly lit, shot the length of the building and off of that what seemed to be dozens of rooms. From these came a humming, people talking in low voices, no words of anger or laughter or even surprise, but things of little personal interest, at least to the employees, although perhaps compelling to the people whose lives were touched.

Louder than this was the metallic clashing sound of manual typewriters, not only the staccato plink-plinking of the key letter levers striking the page, but the long slide of metal on metal as the typewriter carriage was slid across to begin a new line, zing. Plink, plink, zing, and to warn the typist of the approach of the right hand margin, a tinkly bell. Plink, plink, plink, tinkle bell, zing. A cacophony of effort, of paper and letters and secretarial drudgery, producing a result in conformity with the simple and pure heart and desire of Jesus Christ, our Lord and Savior.

The receptionist was away from her desk. I moved quietly down the hall reading the nameplates on each closed door: Father Scully, Confraternity of Christian Dogma; Father Spinelli, Propagation of the Creed; Miss McNab, Secretary to Francis Evelyn Ashcroft; Archbishop Timothy Lehane – bingo – I tried the doorknob – it was locked. I knocked – no answer. But the nameplate next to it was promising: it read Francis Evelyn Ashcroft, Personal Secretary to the Archbishop. I opened the door and peeked in. The room was empty, except for a large desk with a pile of papers on it. I remembered what St. Zeno had said: "The best place for an important letter is with other important letters."

I crept in and slid my letter into the middle of the other letters and asked St. Zeno to take care of it, and left the building as fast as I could.

FRANCIS EVELYN ASHCROFT

IT WOULD BE FOOLISH TO UNDERESTIMATE THE IMPORTANCE of the Chancery Office, the bureaucratic wing of the Archdiocese of San Francisco. Here was the seat of final appeals for matters churchly, accompanying city parishioners from birth to grave - those who lived ordinary, strictly conforming lives but also the stickier cases: babies born in irregular circumstances and unfortunates who entered eternity by their own hand. In no circumstances were judgments withheld. Decisions were made and notice given.

There presided Francis Evelyn Ashcroft, personal secretary to the Archbishop. Among his duties were periodic presentations given in the numerous parishes, his last one an Evening of Recollection at St. Cyril's, three weeks previously. The Archbishop also trusted Francis implicitly in his job of answering the letters of parishioners submitting their problems to ecclesiastical authority for judgment. For ordinary Catholics anything other than official rulings would be spiritual pride. Imagine that, thinking for yourself. So important was Francis that he himself had a secretary, Francis's own job being to safeguard the Archbishop from vexatious correspondence, as his secretary, Miss McNab's, job was to constrict the conduit further down. Between the two of them, the Archbishop, and to lesser extent, Francis, himself, were successfully surrounded by sycophants and thus spared trying situations.

Today Francis felt quite efficient, as indeed he did most days. He applied himself happily to the mound of letters before him at his desk stacked high with his various references, his bastions of authority, as he cited Canon Law, the codified law of the Church; the *Summa Theologica*, the ultimate in medieval thought, and occasionally things that he had read in his mother's "Ladies Home Journal." The unyielding absolutism of the Church was his bulwark:

Daughter to be married in a Protestant church: don't attend. Abandoned by a philandering husband: marriage is for life, no remarriage for you. Died unreconciled with Mother Church: no Catholic burial.

Prospective marriages were halted, erring children cut off and romances snuffed out. Francis loved to be told what to do, and loved telling other people what to do. He didn't mind being at either end of the stick. He was a master and a slave of unapologetic authoritarianism. Francis Ashcroft gave no quarter nor asked for any.

There were more letters. Was there no end? He spent the next hours replying to people begging on account of some terminal illness or other to be included in the Archbishop's next trip to Lourdes (already full up); requests for help with school tuition by mothers recently widowed (sorry, reduced tuition only for families of four or more children); and couples wishing to secure for their wedding day a more attractive church like Old Saint Mary's, instead of their own dowdy parish (tough luck). He had at one point considered being a priest, and while the clerical garb was smart, the foppish streak in him, to be satisfied only by the polka-dot ties he succumbed to while walking through F.W. Woolworth, well, these won out.

Francis had been born to an Anglo-Irish family, barely Roman Catholic, of the lace curtain variety, certainly not shanty Irish. This was evidenced by his middle name, Evelyn, Eve as in Christmas Eve, and it pleased him that only the cognoscenti knew that he shared the name with Evelyn Waugh, author of *Brideshead Revisited*, that masterpiece of the tortured Catholic soul.

He, like the other Evelyn, was an aesthetic Catholic, loving the vestments, tapestries embellished with embroidery, the musty smell of incense, the cryptic mystery of Latin, the flummery and pageantry of the Church. There was a lot to love there. But if the rest of the moral code came with it, that was ok. But poor Francis, he wasn't at all like Waugh's tall, slim, elegant Charles Ryder.

Francis, always Francis, never Frank, was the sort of man of whom it could be said that he'd be better looking if he had a chin. He had, in a way, carried his adolescence into adulthood with him, for he always had a pimple going. His face was a battleground of warring welts and ruptures and this upset him somewhat because of what was generally said about the connection between pimples and some very private sins, but his self-importance, in general, won the day and absolved him of self-consciousness. One little guy, with one little nose and one little chin, with one little willy, with thoughts as inconsequential as pee-water, making final decisions for the faithful.

Francis picked up the next letter. His nose wrinkled and his lips smudged into a pucker of disdain. The frilled, flowing European script did not in the least intrigue him. People he knew did not write that way. All those swirls and loops would require some deciphering. He looked at the signatures: A. Kenny and scribe: H. Klein. These names meant nothing to him. He fell to work and a few minutes later slammed the letter down on his desk top in a rare spot of temper. This woman --- thinking she could get special consideration! The words in reply flew off his pen.

> "The Church holds absolutely to its age old condemnation of intercourse between husband and wife which artificially precludes the possibility of fertility and childbirth. This is clear and irrevocable. It is suggested that the person involved go to confession, for the sacrament of penance not only is cleansing, but can be a great restorative to health of mind and body."

These people with their minds in the gutter, their wanton and lustful ways, Francis was outraged. And suddenly he felt an urge, a swelling netherward, an uprising of his member. His eyelids batted and his breath came quick. The evening was seeping in between the slats in the Venetian blinds, and soon he would be alone in the dark.

A ROUGH NIGHT AND HEAVENLY SWOONS

A CHILD AWAKENS IN THE NIGHT, foreign territory for a young child, and hears as it were a thunder storm, though there is no thunder, is no storm, but only the horrible rumble of muted voices in the next room, alarming her. Words slam back and forth in a man's near shout and a woman's sob –the same long word that is not understood but is spoken again and again. She in the darkness feels only the smooth pillow under her cheek and the rumpled sheets and blankets twisted in the half-heard ordeal and still doesn't cry.

I, wiping my sleepy face with the back of my hand, tumbled out of bed, but quietly so as not to waken my sister, and moved across the unlighted room in its inky blackness, my arms and face and body swimming in the fluid-like dark. What was going on, what was going to happen to me?

I opened the door and stepped into the hall, switching on the light. Blinking against the brightness, I saw my father coming toward me. "Turn off that God damn light and go back to bed." I went back in, but lay down on the thin carpet near the door, straining to see light through the crack at the door's base. But I saw none. I slept. My bones grew sore and my body chilled, and I yearned for comfort. I sneaked back into the hall toward the front room, but the whole house was black. There was then no television to watch, no magazines or books to read, we had no record player. There was just the glow of my father's cigarette, glowing brightly with his inhale, dimly with exhale, like a lighthouse beacon as he sat on the davenport in the dark. I dropped to the floor silently and crawled toward him. I wanted only to be near him, even if unseen. "We'll be all right, sweetie," he said without turning. "Go back to bed."

I WAS A CHILD, TOO INNOCENT TO UNDERSTAND and too powerless to control the forces at work in my family. In need of a refuge I turned to Mother Church. My piety grew.

I got an allowance of 15 cents once a week or maybe every two weeks when things were tight. I had saved 80 cents, an enormous sum, and I decided to bet it all, as some fathers in the parish played the ponies, putting the family's rent money on Bing's Baby, Normandy Gal or Slickeroo. I dropped all 16 nickels into the collection box beneath the statues of the Holy Family, Jesus, Mary and Joseph. They never argued. They just stood there, holding plaster flowers, St. Joseph a rose and Mary, a lily. I wondered if the secret to a happy family was gardening. I knelt before them and prayed as hard as I could. Sister Raymond, in religion lesson, teaching her pupils how to be holy, had made us stare motionless at something, a pinpoint, in front of us, and say over and over again, "Hail Mary, full of grace, the Lord is with thee," "Hail Mary, full of grace," "Hail Mary." From time to time she'd yell "James Lucca, I see your eyes moving" or "Denise Bonier, stop giggling or you'll get a good slap from me." All to make us holy. So it seemed the right thing to do – to pay my 80 cents and stare at the Holy Family statues, repeating the magic words over and over: "Jesus, Mary and Joseph, I give you my heart and my soul," 11, 13, 17 times. St. Teresa of Avila in her heavenly swoons had nothing on me. My concentration grew intense. I wobbled on my knees, the blood left my face, my head spun, and I chipped my tooth on the marble altar rail as I fainted. "The holiness of the dear child," muttered Miss Mulcahy, the mustachioed ironer of altar linen, as she picked me up. "The holiness of the child."

TO FEEL BAD IS TO BE GOOD

To feel bad about my sins,
to feel bad about the sufferings of Jesus,
his agony in Gethsemane, the scourging,
the nailing on the Cross, and everything else, take your pick,
to feel bad about the sorrow of the Blessed Virgin
("at the cross her station keeping,
stood the mournful Mother weeping"),
and finally, always with me,
to feel bad about my mother.

To feel bad was to be good, the supplications of the Litany of the Precious Blood of Jesus rattling around in my head – "Blood of Christ, falling upon the earth in the Agony, have mercy on us, Flowing forth in the Crowning of Thorns, have mercy on us." The picture of the Sacred Heart hanging in our hall, fixing me with a mournful gaze each time I passed, His heart bound tightly round with thorns, fire engulfing it in little pointed licks of flames, His soulful look saying, "You have made me suffer." Certainly other children in the classroom did not feel this way, but I was burdened with a literal turn of mind, and a very orderly mental wiring and, given the constructs, the premises that were drilled into me, when I was wounded and in need, this way of thinking was the rational result.

Both legs had been kicked out from under me, and my native buoyancy had been hobbled and crippled. It was inevitable that I should accept any emotional prosthetic device, however raw and scathingly sensitive its attachment, however painfully cruel, as a promised solution. I saw no other recourse.

PENANCE I

I BEGAN TO GO TO CONFESSION OFTEN. Any sacrament was a way of getting grace and since Holy Orders (becoming a priest) and Extreme Unction (the blessing for the dying) were off-limits to me, confession or Penance seemed a good choice. The trouble was that my sins were inconsequential and I grew tired of reporting missed morning prayers and inattention at Mass. My sister's sins were different. Virgie lived life more vividly than I and I began to confess her sins thinking that she would probably not bother to confess them and so I would do so for her. I went, out of habit, to the confessional box shared by Father Desmond Maloney and Father Miles Landis. You never knew which priest you would get.

> "I stuffed Necco wafers into the Poor Souls' collection box."
>
> "I drew a picture of a fat lady with a big butt in a church missal."
>
> "I took the church bulletins and made paper airplanes out of them."
>
> "I stole a candy bar from Bubble's School Store (everyone knew that only thefts over $2 were mortal sins and candy bars at 5 cents were safe – but were the thefts added up at the end of the year? – a disquieting thought.)

The priests always seemed to perk up when I confessed to Virgie's sins, full of Technicolor detail and dramatic urgency. Today I had an inspiration. It was full of the ring of half truth. "I tied up a neighbor boy in our basement. I used my jump rope." Virgie had done that, but Dougie Robertson was happy enough to stand still and be part of the cowboy and Indian reenactment.

"He didn't mind. No one usually pays attention to him."

"What then?" Father Landis asked eagerly, leaning forward.

"I tried to light his shoes on fire, but they wouldn't light. That's when he started crying."

"Was he crying because they wouldn't light?"

"No, he changed his mind and wanted to go home. But I tried some more – I had lots of matches – but they still wouldn't light."

"Were the shoes leather or rubber?" asked Father Landis.

"Leather."

"Oh, that's the trouble. They would probably take the flame better if they were rubber," said Father Landis ruminatively, becoming for the moment a disappointed co-conspirator.

"Oh well, they didn't catch fire. Jesus didn't weep over this one," he said with a small chuckle. "Go out and play."

"What, what did you say, Father?"

"Just go outside and play, sweetie. The sun's finally melting the fog."

"But what should I say for my penance, Father?"

"Well, let's see. God bless everyone you love and everyone who loves you, living and dead. And say a small prayer for the souls in the flames of purgatory."

What a strange penance. Penances were always in the form of memorized prayers, five Hail Mary's and so on. But I would do what he said and I'd start by saying, "God bless Father Landis."

PENANCE II

TODAY I WAS DETERMINED TO GET ANSWERS. I waited in line outside the confessional booth, having no idea who I'd get, Father Landis or Father Maloney. Father Maloney, or Smokey Maloney as he was called, for the cigarette that perpetually hung out of his mouth. Mrs. Madigan, a neighbor, had remarked to my mother, "The man would say Mass with a cigarette in his mouth if the Bishop would let him." When my mother looked shocked, she had said, "Don't be alarmed, Ann. No one will ever tell him what I said. No one ever tells the priests what they don't want to hear, just what they want to hear." When my mother softly objected, Mrs. Madigan said, "That's why they all think their arse smells sweet," and she roared with laughter to my mother's horror. Mrs. Madigan was another woman on the block that the ladies didn't talk to much. She was plain spoken and her husband was a bartender. She too smoked. In 1946 almost everyone, to some degree, did.

Father Maloney brusquely slid open the wooden panel between penitent and priest. Through the wire screen I saw him make a large sign of the cross over me and say, "In nomine Patris, et Filii, et Spiritis Sancti, Amen." Instantly my side of the booth filled with the smell of cigarettes and another smell, equally repellent, something dark, medicinal, almost sinister. I drew back and stared at the shadow man inches away behind the mesh barrier, his face glowing yellow in the small light, as he sputtered at me in exasperation, "Go on, go on. Other people are waiting."

"Bless me, Father, for I have sinned. It has been a week since my last confession." Then the word that I had heard that night, that I had been practicing, again and again, first thing on getting out of bed, while washing my face and walking to school, again and again. The word that I had heard hurled back and forth between my mother and father, in the black of the night. "I committed contraception." There was an explosion of agitation, and Father Maloney furiously slammed open the screen, and thrust his face, licorice stick hanging from his half open mouth, into my side of the booth, and yelled at me, "You did WHAT?"

The old ladies nodding off in the pews over their rosary beads woke up abruptly, the sacristan replacing the spent candles with fresh ones spun round, and I was out through the curtain of the confessional, down the aisle and across the vestibule and out the heavy front door of St. Cyril's Church, before I stopped and seeing the sun, realized I was safe. Away from the cavern of the church where anything could be said and anything believed. Away from the supernatural where up was down, wide was narrow, where a bread wafer was God, and impossibility was binding doctrine. I skipped down the street in the fresh air, swinging my arms in the sunshine smiling at everyone I met.

REQUIEUM

"QUESTION 473 OF THE BALTIMORE CATECHISM:

What are the blessed objects of devotion most used by Catholics?"

"Answer:

The blessed objects of devotion most used by Catholics are: holy water, candles, ashes, palms, crucifixes, medals, rosaries, relics, scapulars, and images of Our Lord, the Blessed Virgin and the saints."

Committed to memory, mastered, recited word for word, not an item out of sequence. A successful rote execution was worth something, wasn't it?

If I had memorized all five of such catechism question and answers, I would ask Sister Antoinette if I could leave the classroom to go to the 9:00 o'clock Mass. More opportunity to get grace, credit in my spiritual bank account. Grace I was confident I could trade in for favors in the here and now.

The 9:00 o'clock Mass was often a funeral Mass, attended sometimes by a swarm of mourners, black garbed, many in grief, just as many through obligation, others in hopes of a bequest or material advantage, however far-fetched or unlikely.

In the aisle stood two old ladies who, through practice, were especially good at looking piteous, letting their faces go slack jawed and eyes heavenward, hands over heart, extending baskets with holy cards commemorating the birth date and death date with a brief sentimental verse. Miss Mulcahy and Denise's aunt, Miss Bonier, were often asked by the family back to the house afterwards where they ate cake and drank tea, or better yet a little whiskey with lemon and sugar. This made standing all morning in a drafty church in the company of a corpse worthwhile. They were the best St. Cyril's could offer in the way of professional mourners.

The officiating priest would intone from the altar steps, "Requiem aeternam dona eis, Domine, et lux perpetua luceat eis." "Grant them eternal rest, O Lord, and let perpetual light shine upon them." The Latin had a grandeur and dignity that seemed to lift the congregation out of their separate realities of bus fares and umbrellas, overdue books and intimate anger, up into the loftiness of the ersatz Gothic rafters, to the heights where, who knows, dwelt God. We were momentarily transported.

Most of the priests said the same thing at every funeral Mass – why change when the mourners did that for you? There was the usual stuff about how the deceased would be missed, and how sure we all were that eternal life was waiting for them. Death was made to seem just some door, easily opened, where on the other side stood the Blessed Virgin and St. Joseph and a host of saints, their martyred and maimed bodies all neatly bandaged up, cavorting in a welcoming carnival. How certain we were. How nice.

Occasionally, there would be a confusion in that the priest, still sleepy and without his breakfast at 9:00 A.M., would get the sex of the deceased wrong or give a large, appreciative family of children to a spinster whose body had never known man. This was usually corrected by Miss Mulcahy who whispered into the altar boy's ear who then passed the news on to the priest. There was one exception to all this – Father Miles Landis always seemed to have spoken to the family – he knew if a woman was fecund or virginal, or a man, an attorney or a barkeep.

One morning when the congregation was particularly sparse, Father Landis spoke: "Today we mark the death of a man, who though of low station, heeded the call of Christianity with gentleness toward the afflicted, loyalty to the truth and readiness to endure. I ask your prayers for the deceased, Mr. Daniel Eichelberry, who had been in declining health since the death of his best friend Harry last year. Mr. Eichelberry was a purveyor of scrap iron."

I bolted up and cried out, "The Ragman" and as quickly sat down. I hadn't known that the Ragman had a name.

When the funeral parlor pall bearers hoisted the coffin shoulder high and proceeded down the long aisle between the empty pews, trailed by Father Landis, sprinkling holy water on the casket from his wand, I alone followed the coffin, making up the funeral procession. Hadn't the Ragman said, that day on the stairs, that I was his daughter? Tears streaked my face and my lips were clamped to hold in the sobs. I grieved from the heart of me for him and my loss of him.